The Lost Boys of Ladywell

a novel

Aidan Martin

Illustrated by Mark Deans

Guts Publishing

Published by Guts Publishing, 2024

Cover art © 2024 Mark Deans
Cover design © 2024 Julianne Ingles

ISBN 978-1-0687604-0-2 (paperback)
978-1-0687604-1-9 (ebook)

Printed in the UK

www.gutspublishing.com

Raw, frenetic, and funny, *The Lost Boys of Ladywell* is as wild and tragic as any heavy night out. With breathless pace and prose that buzzes off the page, it's a book you can't help but binge. – Callum McSorley, author of *Squeaky Clean* (The McIlvanney Prize 2023)

The characters drip off the page and it immerses you in a world that is fierce and hilarious in equal measure. A truly wonderful example of proletarian fiction that oozes authenticity from its core. Highly recommended. – Colin Burnett, author of *A Working Class State of Mind* and *Who's Aldo?*

What Martin gets spot on is the realism of what life is like for people on the edge of society just trying to get by and feel something in their lives. With elements of Welsh, Kelman, and Bukowski it's one of the best novels of the year. – John Gerard Fagan, author of *Fish Town & Silent Riders of the Sea.*

With a cacophony of words, characters, places, and a plot driven at speed, *The Lost Boys of Ladywell* is not for the fainthearted. The themes of the story are beautifully illustrated by Mark Deans in his striking images which beckon the way in to each chapter, a perfect partner to the stark narration. – Richard Wills, author of *Bloody Social Worker*

PLUR

Peace, love, unity, respect: a mantra embraced by some popular culture communities, especially those associated with rave and electronic dance music events: ravers making new friends in the spirit of PLUR.

This book is a completely fictional storyline with
fictional characters set in the very real world I grew up
in. I have borrowed heavily from characters I grew up
around. But the beauty about fiction is unlike memoir,
you have the freedom to take creative liberties and
mould a story of your own imagination. So, the thing
about *TLBOL* is that some of it is utter fantasy, yet some
of it is as real as it gets.

Aidan Martin

The Lost Boys
of Ladywell

CHAPTER 1
THE SESH

Chapter One: The Sesh

Fuck knows what happened that night. Phil has been missing ever since. Lucas was off his tits and Mikey was gouching hard. I still don't know how it got to this. All I know is my big cuz is gone. Not gone like he sometimes chooses to be. The way Phil loves to fall off the grid during a heavy drug binge. A self-sabotaging pity-party where he starts thinking about how shit the world has been to him. Not that type of gone where he disappears into a void of purple haze and vallies. This time he is GONE.

Before that moment, we were fuckin flying. I had the cash on me. Lucas had the coke. I think Mikey was still poppin his bird's opiates. She'd done her back in falling off a horse. Stupid lassie still doesn't know why her pills kept disappearing. And Phil. Phil was unusually quiet. Maybe because he was nervous about seeing Scott. Scott was his former partner. They weren't into each other. They were DJs. A duo. Well they used to be.

Lucas: "Fuckin cheer up Phil ya miserable cunt!"

We flew down Carnegie Road with Tiësto blaring and Lucas at the wheel. We were on our way to Room At The Top, or what we always called RATT.

The car journey to the raves was part two of the buzz. There were four sections in total.

Part one: pre-rave sesh at the gaff.
Part two: taxi, or drink and drug-drive to the rave.
Part three: the rave.
Part four: the after party.

Part five was the unofficial and unspoken universally accepted section in the drug world. The comedown. But at part two, the drive, no cunt was anywhere near thinking about that. You dealt with the comedown when, and *only* when, it was strangling you into submission.

Anyway, Phil was in denial.

Phil: "I'm fine ya dick. You just drive cuz and geez a few lines back here so I can liven this prick up."

He nudged Mikey, cloudy-headed and chewing his gums already. He thought the rest of us were oblivious to it, as if we were a bunch of dafties. At certain points, we'd catch him staring into space, forgetting where he was, his mind wandering off into a plan to find more opiates. Sometimes his poor auld dear of a granny would be the first port of call for him to pilfer. She was a heavily medicated widow.

Mikey: "Am awrite Phil, fuck sake man, just lookin forward to the night. It's you that's needin livened up. Pure shitting it to see Scott again. And I cannae believe Snez is missing this tonight."

Me: "I tried calling him all week, but he didnae answer."

Snez was our other mate. Our funny, ginger pal. He dipped in n out a lot. At the moment he had dipped out.

I was snorting lines in the passenger side next to Lucas, my big brother, who was flying, both literally and figuratively. My buzz was taking flight with missile-like-precision, but my thoughts were veering into less comfortable territory. Meeting Rab and Sunny in the middle of a trance night seemed both genius and ridiculous. Less chance of getting jumped there, I thought. Maybe I could sort things out with them. Maybe I could stop Lucas from pouncing on them. The fact Scott was playing this gig was just the way shit had landed. He was hoping to make things right with Phil. I worried Lucas might have other ideas though.

Lucas: "Nathan, dinnae be greedy, pass some lines to the schmucks in the back."

The music shook the doors of his blue Ford Fiesta. In fact the entire interior of the car vibrated so hard it felt like it was as buzzing as us. I took a fat line for myself, right up the tunnel of my twenty-pound note. Zooooop! Aaaaah. That fucking hit the spot man.

Me: "Here we go boys!"

The elation in my voice matched my eyes, like a children's space hopper bouncing up and down.

Mikey: "So what's the plan then lads?"

He was finally coming alive. Quality gear like that could bring even the likes of Frankenstein out of himself.

Mikey: "Like how we goin about all this?"

My brother Lucas always had simple answers:

"Deal wae they two cunts, then the DJ cunt, charlie, birds, party!"

Laughter erupted, like giggling clowns on speed.

Mikey: "Naw seriously man, I don't trust that Sunny prick one bit like. I dinnae understand what his problem is."

Mikey gulped his MD 20/20. Truth was no one trusted them. Rab or Sunny that is. But we either sorted it out with them or things were going to kick off big time. My brawny coke buzz swung me in and out of reality. I had my window down and was sipping on the cold air rushing into the car as we sped down the motorway. The Mad Dog going around provided an extra edge.

When the next track came on, 'Ayla,' the DJ Taucher mix, the mood in the car changed instantly, like we all plugged in to one big electric socket. I bit my bottom lip, closed my eyes, and cut shapes with my hands. Tracks like this were travel guides for your dunt. Showing your dunt the fastest way to climax. No need for any luggage or baggage. Four dunts on a one-way excursion. Phil started cheering the way only a former DJ could.

Phil: "Yaaassss. Aww this fuckin tune lads. This fuckin tune."

Suddenly Phil was back. The worry gone from his face. The four of us were high as fuck, all suited n booted as if we'd just done a smash n grab at River Island. We lived for this shit man. It's all we had.

Mikey was fully functional now, his need for an opiate top-up delayed for a few more hours. That charlie was proper strong gear like. He was kissing Phil's head in the back of the motor, both of them laughing. I looked

4

over at Lucas with a crazy unpredictable look on his face. His green rebel eyes and that cheeky smirk crept up his face. Just as the tune hit its peak Lucas screamed: "Yeeehaaaa fucksticks" and slammed his foot to the floor in that battered old Fiesta. With my stomach spinning and tossing with excitement, this was my favourite place to be. Right on the fucking edge alongside my boys.

It was November and that murky, Scottish darkness added to the 'fuck it' mood. We pulled up outside the club, seeing all the other revellers parked up in their ecstasy. It was like everyone was in love. The buzz from inside was drifting out. People were screaming with excitement. Lads piggybacking on top of their mates, acting like dafties, pure buzzing. Lassies screaming "wooooooo" bobbing their heads from side to side, holding tins of beer, high as fuck. Some were still in their cars drinking with their tunes blaring, smoking joints and popping eccies. Some were already on their bottles of water, streaming with sweat. We could feel the beat from the gig rumbling in the ground.

As we approached a rampant queue to enter, we polished off our Mad Dog and Stellas and Phil finished a joint. Lucas slapped his hands together with just the right amount of rage.

"Let's fuckin do this!"

Walking up to the line leading to the bouncers, anxiety peaked. No one could stomach the idea of getting KB'd from a gig. If you looked too out of it you ran that risk. Or if you came across a bouncer with small-dick syndrome he might try to make an example out of you. You always had to have the right blend of not acting like

5

a prick but not showing any weakness. Or be a gorgeous lassie in a short skirt. That did wonders with *some* pervy bouncers. Most of them were sound though, and typically a good source of eccies too.

Phil: "Try no swing yer jaw for five minutes Mikey so we can actually get in, eh skinnybaws."

Phil gave that wheezy, cackling laugh of his. He really did have the voice of a thousand fags.

Lucas: "Aye it will be them cunts with all the gear anyway man!"

Two burly men with walkie talkies, bald heads and crappy neck tattoos waved us through. They didn't give a fuck about us anyway. They were too busy looking for those desperate girls that clung to bouncers like flies on shit.

Rain was spitting down as we entered. I could hear a muffled version of 'Castles in the Sky' by Iain Van Dahl from inside. Everyone was already buzzing off their tits singing: "The roof, the roof, the roof is on fire!" or "Here we, here we, here we fuckin go!"

After hugging a good few elated strangers we made our way inside. Flashing lights broke up the darkness. Reds. Greens. Blues. Like a rave rainbow. Girls had luminous furry boots and bright fishnets with glowing necklaces and bracelets. Some of them dyed their hair like candy floss, matching their sparkly face paint. Pierced bellybuttons with wee charms dangling from skimpy wee outfits everywhere and pierced tongues as well. All luminous. Guys had their whistles and glow sticks. Some even wore jump suits whilst others alternated between their best shirts, baggy t-shirts, or jumpers. A few girls had loose ties over their outfits like Avril Lavigne.

Oh and the odd twats in fedoras wound Lucas up a lot. Middle-class guys who wanted to hang with the scheme rats for a night. Lucas thought they were pretentious cunts. I had to agree with him. Phil felt the same way. He didn't like the scene being infiltrated by tourists. Felt it was a massive disrespect. Anyway we were inside and that's all that mattered.

There were three massive rooms with different sets on. Each one had its own bar and its own theme name too. I guess it was more fun than calling them rooms one, two and three. Instead the rooms were called Aqua, Moonlight and Silk.

In the middle was the 'quiet spot' where you would take someone if you had a big ecstasy moment and were full of love. Usually a one-nighter.

ATB's '9pm till I come' blared from one of the rooms. We gathered in a tactical huddle.

Me: "Where youz wantae go first?"

Mikey: "Let's go into Moonlight."

His eyes darted about following two girls walking in that direction. Scott was due on in Aqua in about an hour, and Rab n Sunny were going to text me when they made it in. So we had some time and went with Mikey into Moonlight.

We merged into a crowd of sweaty ravers. Lasers flashed pink and purple. Lilac smoke hung at the top of the ceiling. The buzz was real and intense. I could smell singe, as if someone had just set fire to a couch. But it was a fantastic smell. The music was so loud we had to shout and grab each other by the neck. Paul Oakenfold pounded through our bodies, 'Southern Sun.'

I swear to God we felt every word.

After a period of blissful bouncing, 'Dark and Long' by Underworld came on. I'd always loved this track since I heard it in *Trainspotting*. I found myself getting emotional. Looking at us all. Phil was twenty-eight now. A perennial drug user with a fertile imagination. His natural habitat was close to the edge.

But everyone loved Phil. Maybe it was the way his eyes made his whole face smile. Or how he could make you believe in even the wildest dreams. Phil was always webbing a protective layer of humour around himself. Charming everyone. But I knew he was gutted. He'd left a trail of wreckage behind him where all his potential used to be. Failed marriage. A baby daughter he didn't see. Dishonourably discharged from the army. Failed DJ. His old partner Scott making it big where it could have been them both. He was a broken boy from a broken family.

It wasn't just him who felt broken. We all did man. Phil said we all came from a 'broken generation.' We might not have been boys anymore, but we weren't quite men either. Not one of us had a biological father in our lives. Our dad left Lucas and I when we were kids. And Mikey, he was the oldest of eleven. His mother bled her fingers and toes working three jobs, whilst their dad fucked off.

And there it was! Tiësto, 'Adagio for Strings.' If ever there was an emotionally provocative trance track, this was it. I focused in on Mikey. Stupid cunt didn't even realise he had model looks. And I don't just mean the skinny frame from the opiates he was munching like Smarties. See growing up was rough for a kid from a big family in a housing scheme. He had a coo's lick, damaged teeth and wore glasses that magnified his eyes. He got bullied at school and his dad was a useless prick. Showed him nothing but hate before he fucked off. But Mikey was different now. He'd worked on himself. Took out loans he couldn't afford to buy himself perfect teeth and contact lenses.

Like the rest of us he grew up in streets where you had to fight to survive. Schools where you had to fight to survive. You hit first or you got battered. Nothing but war wounds and reminders from teachers about all the jobs we would never get, spinning round our heads.

I kept looking at my best pal as he danced with Phil and Lucas. And I knew that as much as his appearance had changed, and gave him a touch of arrogance, it was a front for all his insecurities. He lived for nights like this though. We all did.

The music changed pace with 'Meet her at the Love Parade' by Da Hool.

My brother Lucas was the hardest shell to crack. At twenty-five he acted like he gave no fucks about anything. He'd sooner take a hit to the face to protect one of us than offer a hug, if you know what I mean. That's how he showed his love. He was combustible but it was always with good intentions. Whereas I was the opposite. Overly emotional and always fearing the worst. I got slagged often for greeting on the eccies.

I mean let's get it straight, neither one of the four of us had fuck all to look forward to. All we had was each other. And drugs. And Trance. *Trance*.

I was twenty-two and already in deep with the charlie. But I reminded myself it was 'under control' and I was still young enough to be considered a young guy with a future.

I didn't really know too much about myself.

Mikey was twenty-two as well by the way. We didn't just go through school together. We got paper rounds at the same corner shop together. Got sales assistant jobs in that very shop. Robbed the place blind together. Porn mags, power cards, fags, and bottles of voddy. Then went to work for a dodgy debt collection company. Alongside Lucas, Phil and Snez—our friend who was missing in action—we were tight as fuck.

Just as my drug-induced daydream was in full swing my pocket vibrated. Rab and Sunny were here. Sunny texted: "That's us in Aqua. Get us at the bar."

Lucas and Phil were in the zone, having a love-in on the dancefloor under pulsating strobe lights with lilac smoke drifting between them.

I grabbed Mikey and shouted in his ear.

Me: "That's Rab and Sunny here man. Don't say a word to Lucas. Am gonnae go speak to them. See if I can sort this shit out."

Mikey: "No fuckin way man, we all go!"

Me: "No brother, it will all kick off if we pile in. Just trust me. Let me deal with this."

He knew I was serious but seemed edgy as fuck at the idea. I nodded in the direction of two girls on the dancefloor. Fucking hell, I could see why Mikey had his eyes on them.

Me: "Go chat them up then Mikey. Show us what you've got. I'll be back before you know it."

Oh he liked *that* idea alright. I just hoped he was going to leave the blonde for me. God damn she was tidy.

I darted out without saying a word to Phil or Lucas. On my way out I watched as Mikey approached the two birds. But fuck me the nerves were back. Last time I saw Rab and Sunny they were waving knives at me.

Aqua was just as jumping. Turquoise smoke spiralled over blue-green techno lasers. I spotted Sunny at the bar. Typical fuckin Sunny. Standing there, wearing his black designer T-shirt with white patterns dotted all over it and a gleaming, thick gold chain hanging out. His cropped black hair was rock hard with gel and the sides were shaven with a star-pattern. Matched with two vertical lines shaved into his right eyebrow and a diamond stud earing in his left ear.

Sunny was an Asian-Scottish lad I'd known since we were kids. Before he became a cardboard gangster driving about in a supped up Subaru, he was just a normal boy.

I was looking for that prick Rab. He was the real danger out of the two of them. A hothead with a short fuse. I clocked him just behind Sunny getting in beers. He was in his triple denims and brown Rockport boots with his long, shaggy blonde hair bouncing all over the place. He spotted me and struck those eyes upon me. I tried to have a bit of swagger, but there was ice in my veins. Sweat beaded on my forehead and it wasn't the coke.

Me: "Y'awrite lads?"

I couldn't hide my insincerity. Rab cut holes in me with his eyes.

Sunny: "Aye no bad mate."

He looked over my shoulder to see if I came with anyone then leaned into me, his mouth like a tumble dryer, gnawing his chewing gum.

Sunny: "Listen Nathan. I didnae want any of this shit. But you fucked us."

I nodded as my eyes popped out of my skull. I knew fine well Sunny was testing me. One click of his fingers, and I'd be gutted like a dead pig right where I stood. Rab watched on as we all pretended they weren't just trying to skewer me to death a week ago.

Me: "Look, I've got three-hundred n fifty quid on me. Lucas has a quarter bag on him. That fucking tides us over for now man –"

Rab: "Bullshit!"

He spat venom like a gila monster then shoved his forehead into my nose. Sunny half-heartedly stuck his left arm in between us.

Rab: "Fuckin let's go Nathan!"

Just as I was wondering how to get out of this debacle I noticed something from my peripheral vision. It was Scott, stood there with his signature black Ray-Bans on! Scott was otherwise known as Sensei Sounds. That was his DJ stage name. Dinnae ask.

He was prepping some of his gear next to the main stage, with an entourage. At first I thought this could be a good thing. I mean we had been friends at *one* time in our lives. But then I panicked. Phil would be there any minute.

Which meant Lucas too. Last thing I needed was for things to escalate.

'Strange World' by Push was playing. Everyone was bouncing around, and I still had Rab up in my face.

Me: "Listen Rab fuck sake man. Calm down. You gave us a shit fucking batch last month. What did you think we were going to do with it?"

Sunny: "You should have called us Nathan. We could have sorted it out. No fuckin way you just binned it mate. No buying it pal."

Me: "So you no want this cash then?"

I pulled out three-hundred-and-fifty quid rolled up in twenties n' tens. It was nowhere near what I owed them. Rab grabbed it from my hand then screamed in my face again.

Rab: "Is that it?! Get the fuckin rest."

Right on time I saw Phil waltzing into Aqua winking at lassies on the way. Lucas and Mikey weren't with him though. I had no time to figure it out. I made a desperate plea.

Me: "Right stay here I'll go and get the rest. Just wait."

I slowly edged away and to my surprise they let me. Sunny tapped the face of his gold watch and Rab was merely that finger click away from tearing me up. I looked over to see Phil and Scott awkwardly embrace near the main stage.

I went searching for Lucas but couldn't find him anywhere. I paced back and forward through the crowds and popping tunes, looking. Eventually in desperation I ended up in the only room I hadn't checked yet. Silk. The vibe was much the same. Red and orange lasers, loved-up humans cutting shapes on the dancefloor, and yellow smoke being pumped into the crowd. I weaved in and out but alas, no Lucas. I turned to leave before noticing something that caused me to stop dead in my tracks.

Mikey was in Silk chatting up that blonde! Something pierced through my gut. I used to tease him when we were in high school about not being able to get a bird like I could. But he had somehow blossomed and overtaken me. Mikey always got the birds first now.

Bobbing my head from side to side I was half dancing, acting wide, as I gained in on them. I tilted my head back and eyeballed Mikey as if to say to him "c'mon tae fuck man she was mine" but he just screwed his face and pulled a warped smile as if to reply, "she was fair game mate."

Just then *she* turned around and I swear to God just as the DJ fired on 'Beautiful' by Matt Darey, she winded me with her smile. I'm in love and it wasn't the eccy I popped hours before. I felt like I couldn't breathe as I took her in, her smile wide and sexy. Vibrance permeated from her. She stretched the corner of her mouth ever so gently and said: "Hey."

I think I was hypnotised and forgot how to speak as I stared into her brown eyes. She was curvy and fuck me she wore it well.

Me: "Where you from then? You dinnae sound Scottish to me!"

It was all I could think to say. Typical dickhead move. By now I'd well and truly forgotten the two rabid dogs waiting for me in the other room.

14

New love of my life: "Joburg ya cheeky bastard."

She laughed all high pitched and sexy. God damn even her laugh floored me.

Me: "Where the fuck is that then? Down south?"

She just pissed herself laughing and her brunette pal bent over holding her stomach in hysterics. I didn't think it was that funny to be fair. Mikey formally introduced me to Cassie—the new love of my life—and her mate Erica.

More pressing matters were at hand though.

Me: "Where's Lucas?"

Mikey: "I thought he was still wae Phil? Have you spoke to those pricks yet?"

Me: "Of course I fuckin have that's why am looking for Lucas. He cannae be wae Phil. Phil's wae Scott."

Mikey: "Shit!"

He pulled out his phone to call Lucas. No reply.

Me: "He's no gonnae hear it in here man. Just stay here I'll go look for him."

By this point I could barely stomach the idea of leaving Mikey with Cassie. But I was running out of time. I had no real plan. I needed to ask Lucas what to do next.

Me: "Here Mikey. A wee gift for you."

I handed him a little baggy containing some goodies, hoping to distract him. Mikey accepted and I went back on the hunt.

I stormed about everywhere looking for Lucas. My Nokia was blowing up with texts from Sunny. My mind was all over the shop: 'Shit. Fuck sake. How am I going to sort this shit out and get back before Mikey pulls Cassie?'

15

I was gonnae have to face the music. Literally. I still owed these cunts near enough a barrel of ching.

I was doing the hard man strut as I waltzed back into Aqua. Puffed my chest out. Made myself look dangerous like one of those poisonous frogs from the Amazon rainforest. In my mind I was hyping myself up: 'Show these cunts! Get them fuckin telt!' Just as my bravado was on the up I saw something that made me mouth the word "fuck" to myself.

Phil and Scott were arguing up at the main stage. It looked heated. Some kind of Marcel Woods mix was playing. But they were beyond animated with each other. I could tell that much. I imagined how it was playing out.

Phil: "You fucked me over Scott. It should have been the two of us."

Scott: "Fuck you ya waster. If you spent as much time working on our projects as you did smoking weed you would have been up there with me."

Phil: "You fuckin owe me man. You backstabbing cunt."

Scott: "Fuck you man if anything you owe me for all those no-shows whilst you were melted to pavements oot yer face on jellies!"

My safety net was gone, and their argument was drifting off behind the stage. I couldn't even go and have Phil's back. I had to sort this shit out. Sunny and Rab were staring me down as I got closer to them.

Their numbers had multiplied. There were about seven guys with them. Alright I exaggerate. Three guys. But they were still a mob, experienced and vicious. Fucking hell. I was proper bricking it now.

Me: "Listen –"

BOOM! Some fucker smashed a glass bottle right down the side of my head. I slumped to the floor like a sandbag. A crowd swarmed around me. I attempted a backwards army crawl through an obstacle course of heavy kicks, flashes of light, and thunder bolts of pain. I desperately looked around for Phil, but he was gone.

I was getting the living shit kicked out of me!

I don't know if it was bouncers, or other revellers but somehow, someone pulled me out, and as soon as I had wriggled free I bolted towards the main stage. I stumbled and fell to my knees but didn't look back. I just kept crawling forward, under legs, in between people. My breathing was out of control as I tried to catch a gulp. Some lad looked down at me and shouted "waaaheeey" as I crawled underneath him, thinking this was me having a laugh.

I dragged myself behind the stage. There was only one exit – a long grimy corridor to my right. I thought I could see Phil.

It was hard to focus. The music was hitting me in distorted chunks. I peered back at the crowd scanning it for danger then recoiled. It looked like it was all kicking off now. People were running in all directions, even outside of Aqua.

My mind couldn't process it all: 'What the fuck is going on? Surely that's not because of what just happened?' A member of staff scarpered across the dancefloor, dodging people, carrying a wee green first aid box.

I kept looking around. I couldn't see Sunny or Rab. But I urgently needed to get out of there. I glanced back down the corridor. Two lads were pummelling each other.

'That *is* Phil. He has his hands around Scott's throat! Shit!'

They were attacking each other like animals. I staggered towards them. I kept looking over my shoulder for Rab and Sunny, palming the brick walls to hold me up. I followed the sound until I reached the room. The music from the gig sounded more distant by now and the corridor was void of human bodies. Just us three. I was almost at them and readying myself to pounce on that smarmy bastard Scott as I reached the steel door, with a solitary square window. But then **it** captured my attention, making me stand like a ghostly figure peering through the glass.

'Is *that* what it looks like?' I asked myself in disbelief.

That distraction cost me dearly as the riveted metal slammed into my face with Phil and Scott tumbling out of the room. They kept rolling down the corridor as I tended to my busted-up face once again. Blood covered my hands. I placed them back on my face to delay the rush of pain. 'Fuck that hurt!' Peeking through my fingers, I seen **it** again. Just sitting there!

Unbeknown to me, events were kicking off in the Silk room too. Lucas noticed all the commotion from the quiet spot where he'd been killing some girl with his tongue. He rushed over to Silk as fast as he could, following a staff member with a wee green first aid box who was headed that way.

18

Lucas: "What the fuck is happening? Who the fuck are youz?"

He screamed the questions at Cassie and Erica as he dove to the floor in confusion.

"Oh my God, oh my God. He was fine a minute ago. I don't know what's wrong with him!" Cassie shrilled as Mikey lay convulsing on the floor with purple lips and his body going stiff. Erica wasn't laughing anymore. The staff member was checking Mikey's breathing. Lucas pulled him out the way and lifted his head. A shallow, raspy sound dragged out of his mouth. His eyelids flickered.

Lucas slapped his face: "C'mon man. C'mon. Fuckin c'mon. Mikey! Call a fuckin ambulance. Get some help. Fuck man, Fuck. Mikey!"

People scrambled about in chaos. Lucas looked everywhere for Phil, and me in the crowds. Reluctantly he let the first aider take over.

Fuck knows how much time passed by the time Lucas found me. All I can recall was his lips moving in front of my face. He was asking me where our cousin Phil was. He said no one could find him. Everything crawled. I was dazed.

Lucas held my face in his hands: "Whoooooo dooooone thiiiiiis toooo YOU? Waaaaas it those pricks?"

Me: "Done what?"

Lucas quickly dragged me outside into darkness and cold air. At least the music stopped pounding in my head. It was replaced with a wiry ringing in my ears. Lucas handed me his car keys and shook me by the shoulders.

Lucas: "I need to go with Mikey. Nathan! —he shook me some more— Fuckin listen to me bro! Take the car and follow us!"

But the words shot past me.

Lucas jumped into the ambulance with Mikey, who was laid out on a stretcher with an oxygen mask strapped to his face. I was watching it happen but my grasp on reality was distorted. Just before Lucas sped away in the ambulance he shouted down:

"Where the fuck is Phil?"

CHAPTER 2
THE COMEDOWN

Chapter Two: The Comedown

With my left eyelid hanging down like a broken shutter, I squinted through my right eye. I stood in the overcrowded kitchen of a stranger. I mean we declared our love for each other many times in the last few hours. In between chewing the walls like. We were brothers now. But with the cotton mouth taking full effect, the conversation was drying up. The eccy dunt long gone. My nose was so full of hardened cocaine it felt like cement.

Now that the drugs were wearing off reminders came with flashes of the rave. The crusty dried-up blood all over my face and shirt told the story of the weekend. I didn't think it went too well with Rab and Sunny.

I felt so cold my shoulders were buckling, and my hands were jittery. Suddenly I felt black as fuck. I wanted to cry. The murderous headache sealed the listless doom. Emotional hangover settled in right next to a boaky alcoholic one.

I took my phone out to check my texts. But the battery was dead. I kept forgetting. No cunt in there had a Nokia charger. I needed Lucas to come and get me. My head was on me again: 'How's he going to do that when I've got his car keys? And more to the point, *why* have I got them?'

"So anyway man, am gonnae fuckin do it like. Eeeeeh. I reckon all I need is six grand and I'll have enough to be up and running. Gonnae call it Cheeko's cabs," explained the stranger with the patchy black beard, speaking at a hundred miles an hour. He'd been telling me about his business plan for twelve hours as we snorted lines in his kitchen. The house was a shithole, and until the drugs wore off I believed wholeheartedly in his business acumen. But the comedown was on its fucking way man.

Me: "Aye mate. I told you man. I know you're gonnae do this."

Frantic beardy guy: "And the fuckin great thing is, eeeeh, mate, am gonnae make you one of my top drivers man!"

He ran his thick, hairy-knuckled hands up and down his beard. He had the eccy stutters though. Kept involuntarily making this "eeeeeh" noise.

Didn't matter anyway. I was starting to feel like it was about time to pass out. I needed to get the fuck out of there. Comedowns were remote and lonely and not to be shared with strangers. Salty tears were already camped out in their glands waiting for the internal misery to kick in and invite them down. That's when I asked myself: 'Where am I?'

I stepped over passed out bodies in the hallway as I followed my inner toilet compass. Bathrooms were one of the first areas you scoped out in a strange pad and even in your worst state you still knew how to get back to them.

On route my surroundings came into better focus. There was no wallpaper on the walls of this house. No carpets on the floor. All I could hear from the living room as I approached was the sound of 'Children' by Robert Miles being played. I popped my head in. Some of the survivors were sitting bobbing their heads, looking fiercely depressed. They weren't wearing socks. Pretty sure I'd seen two of them at the back of the room by a fishbowl feeding base to the goldfish and laughing nonsensically earlier in the sesh. Two floating blobs of shimmering orange confirmed my suspicions.

The bog was about as small as a kitchen cupboard. Typical. No soap. No toilet roll. No towels. There was about a hundred dead flies on the windowsill. I splashed cold water all over my face turning the sink a brownish pink as the dried blood washed off. Then I looked into a tiny wall mirror. My eyes were bloodshot red, and my skin was so pale it looked grey. I wiped my hands down my jacket. I felt something strange: 'What the fuck is *that* in my pocket?' I pulled it out to investigate.

My eyelids sprang open. I was talking to myself again: 'How do I have *that*?'

I shoved it back in my pocket at lightning speed. I tried to catch a breath and took out my phone to call Lucas.

Me: "Fuck sake! The stupid cunting battery is dead. I need to get out of here."

I was hoping for a quick escape but the frantic guy with the beard found me again. We'd been glued to each other for what seemed like days. He had two long fishing rods tucked under his arm.

Frantic beardy guy: "Wantae go through to Linlithgow Loch and catch some fish man?"

He was dead serious. I'd done tons of shit like this on eccies man. I wanted out of there, but it wasn't as easy as it sounded trust me. Escaping would be tricky.

Each person that leaves a 'party' like that destroys the buzz the rest of them are trying to hold onto. I mean solidarity and unity are vital when trying to stave off a comedown. You'd end up planning all sorts to get more cash and more drugs. Fuckin re-mortgage your grannies house by the time you're done. But I felt like an empty paper bag. I'd used up all my denial. So I lied.

Me: "Am away to get fags n vodka man. I'll be back in ten minutes. Then we can go fishing."

The beardy guy was buzzing like a wee kid now and went looking for wellies. Soon as he clunked his way upstairs I stumbled out the front door. The wind and rain blew the comedown right into my face. Now came the real question: 'I might have Lucas's car keys but where the fuck is his car?'

I looked up and down the street. I was vaguely familiar with this part of Livi. I wandered with my head tucked down into my chest, trying to protect my face from the rain. Every now and then I peeked up like a swimmer does, to see if I could spot the motor. Finally I spotted it half on a kerb and half over two spaces in a diagonal fashion.

I had no memory of driving there.

I needed to get home before I passed out.

I sagged into the driver's seat and started the engine. Tiësto screamed at me as soon as I turned the key. I felt far too bleak for such uplifting trance. I opened the glove box and found an Ibiza chill disc and stuck it on the CD player before screeching off in a hurry. The window wipers were on full pelt as rain hammered the windscreen.

I blasted up the heating as the relaxing, yet hauntingly beautiful vibe of 'Café del mar' by Energy 52 played. I tried to ignore the lump the size of a small rock rising in my throat. Then the comedown axed its way out like a fanatic. I dissolved into hysterics.

I just fucking hated when trance nights were over. When the drugs wore off and real-life resumed. When all your pain came flooding back, dragging new pain with it. As the track poured into my soul and flowed through my body I couldn't stop the thoughts flooding in too.

I could see my grandad lying in his hospital bed. His skin was a sickly jaundice. He felt rubbery to touch, like it wasn't really him. I could see Lucas crumbling in my arms. Crumbling in a way I'd never seen him before. I've never seen him that way ever again in fact. I was a teenager who didn't know what to do. At one point I was even holding my big brother up in a role reversal that didn't register properly. His screams pierced through me like bullets. They were blood curdling. It was almost as shocking as Grandad lying there dead.

"What do you mean? What do you mean? What do you *mean*?!" were the only words Lucas repeated over and over that day. What neither of us understood, what neither of us could articulate, was what we really lost.

That man was more like our father. Especially to Lucas. We never knew pain like it before.

It was a twelve-minute track. I thought about Phil up on the grand stage with Scott. Scott had black Ray-Bans on, but Phil had yellow-tinted shades. Phil was sticking his pierced tongue out, screaming as the crowd below showed him the kind of love he was searching for his whole life. He had on our grandad's bunnet. It was left to Phil. He was the first grandchild after all.

I was halfway home. Still bawling my eyes out.

I thought about Mikey. Awww Mikey man. We'd been through it all together. Fought against other lads together. Pulled birds together. Took drugs together. There was nothing we hadn't been through. If some cunt started with me they had Mikey in their face. If some cunt started with Mikey they had me in their face. If we were both in the shit then they had Lucas to deal with. And when our pal Snez was around he'd be in our corner too.

See Mikey and I, we left school with fuck all. Just like everyone else where we came from. We had each other's backs. No matter what.

But it felt like we were drifting apart. The opiates man, they were changing him. He would tell me sometimes he felt so high he didn't even know if his eyes were open. It didn't help that he was obsessed with the film *The Matrix*. He spent his days trying to figure out the reality of the world when the truth was he had no handle on what was happening in his own head. He'd lost his sense of humour and was starting to forget things. He clung to Lucas a lot. Like the big brother he never had.

I didn't know what my place was anymore. I didn't have a fucking clue who I was supposed to be. I wondered where my dad was. All these years and nothing. The only thing I ever looked forward to, was our trance nights. But I had secrets. Real secrets. I couldn't tell them. They would never understand. Phil would. Maybe one day I would tell Phil. One day I'd face up to it.

I made it to my street.

As I meandered in the door, I stripped off and stuck my phone on charge. My comedown hit hard. So I fired on a compilation CD. It might not have been the best idea, as I passed in and out of consciousness to the sound of 'As The Rush Comes' by Motorcycle.

I couldn't hear my phone coming back to life over the music. As the charge fuelled through it, text messages came one after one. RATATATA off my bedside table. Voicemail notifications. RATATATA. I lay there oblivious in my single bed under my *Teenage Mutant Ninja Turtle* covers.

Your mind leaps off a cliff in these moments and lands in all sorts of places. It got to a point where I really couldn't tell if I was asleep or awake anymore as I rolled around my bed trying to switch off my coke brain. I was still hallucinating. Seeing all kinds of visions and flashbacks from RATT. My covers were stuck to my sweaty body.

I can't tell you how long I lay there for. It could have been hours or days.

RATATATATA. RATATATA. RATATATA.

Holy fucking shit. My phone was a blizzard of texts. That's when the reality kicked in. I hadn't made it into work. It was Monday afternoon. Fuck! Dread was crawling up my arms as I lifted the mobile to dial my voicemail.

"Eh, hi Nathan. It is Graham Stewart here. Your team leader," he said like I didn't know who the cunt was. "I am just wondering if you plan on making it into work today. We haven't heard from you. Can you check in please? Even just to let us know you are OK."

Delete. Next Voicemail.

"Hi Nathan. It's Graham here again –"

Delete. Next.

"Nathan I am very concerned now. This is not good working practice."

What an unbearable cunt.

I was just about done listening to his pish and ready to delete the voicemail when his next question made me sit upright in my bed.

"Oh and by any chance have you seen your little partner in crime? Michael hasn't showed up today either. It doesn't take a rocket scientist to work out what's going on."

I dropped my phone.

Mikey! I started thumbing through my texts. Holy fuck. I didn't know where to start. The abuse from Sunny or the rants from Lucas asking where I was. I was skim reading them all.

"At A&E now."

"When you coming?"

"Where is my fuckin car bro?"

"Bro what the fuck?"

"Nathan have you seen Phil?"

"Where you at bro?"

"Where the fuck is Phil?"

I was remembering all sorts. It was too much to decipher. Thoughts scrambling over one another fighting to be heard.

Paul Van Dyk's 'For an Angel' was blaring. I looked over at the jacket hanging from my computer chair. I focused on the pocket. Fucking hell. How the fuck did I end up with *that*? I didn't even want to go near it.

I had messages from an unknown number on my phone.

"Hey is your friend OK?"

"Hey, please let me know. We're so worried about him."

"Why you not replying?"

'Fuckin hell. Is that….is that Cassie?' My face lit up. I didn't recall giving her my number.

Sunny sent me a few too. This one summed it up:

"This isnae over ya wee dobber!"

I hadn't even pulled myself out of bed yet. I didn't know where to begin. I had no idea how long I even managed to rest up. There was only one thing for it. Time to text Ben. Also known as Gumball. Gumball was my main coke dealer. He was a bit of a fanny, but he gave me good tick.

Me: "Mate I need 3 grams on tick for 2 weeks. I'll chuck in an extra ten spot if you can bring me a bottle of Bucky round."

Gumball: "Nae bother mate. Geez half an hour."

Thank fuck for Gumball.

I jumped out of the shower feeling more refreshed and less bullied by the comedown.

I moved into the living room to prep for the charlie coming. By prep I meant get a card ready to chop it up and a wee straw to snort the goods. The living room was nothing remarkable. Ancient couch, colour long since faded away. Old box TV in the corner covered in thick dust, with a long metallic arial on top of it which rarely picked up any channels. Plain wooden rectangle table in the centre of the room. Plain walls. No pictures other than one of me and Lucas looking worse for wear at a New Year's Eve party. And windows looking out onto the scheme. I'd never washed them, so it was a kind of blurry, smudged view of the street. My kitchen was practically an extension of the living room with all the basic white goods I received as part of the homeless package from the council. Oh and it went without saying there was a portable CD player on the bunker top.

Gumball finally arrived with my treasure. The Bucky was nicely chilled. I gulped it down and opened the baggy and looked at that beautiful white, powdery rock. The instantly recognisable smell hit me first. Right up my nostrils. It was glorious. Made a puddle form on my tongue. I crushed the rock using an expired provisional driver's license, kept now purely for this purpose, and made a couple of fat ones. But before I touched it, I had to put on the track. *The* track. To me this was *the* trance track.

Mauro Picotto – 'Lizard.'

The first time I ever heard this track was in Lucas's car. It literally changed my life forever. I knew in that moment that trance was my God. As the Faithless song explains, God is a DJ.

I clicked it into my CD player and pressed play.

My brainwaves danced in euphoria. A wee rave inside my skull. I started bopping my head up and down. Clenched my fists and felt the power. The spiral of bucky and trance blending as one, about to be lit on fire by the cocaine. Just as the track approached the peak, I unclenched my fists, raised up my arms at either side of me with my hands opened, palms facing outward, and tilted my head back. Fuccccckkkkk. What a rush! Zoooooop! Extra fat line right up my beak as I needed a reward to kickstart me.

Me: "You want a line Gumball?"

Gumball: "Naw mate I need tae shoot back to the site."

Gumball was a builder or some shit. Quite high up the ranks too. He still made more money from dealing charlie though. I dabbled myself like until it went tits up with Sunny and Rab. But Gumball knew the big dream of two kids and a mortgage wasn't gonnae happen unless he wanted to live in dire straits. So that's what he did. He hid it well. To anyone else his life was monotonous. So no cunt suspected a thing. But I've seen the big piles of cash in his kitchen drawers and all the fancy gadgets in his four-bedroom house. I've met his stupid fiancée who pretends she doesn't live the high life off the back of people like me. The way she speaks down to me as if my coke habit didn't benefit her life. Stupid bitch.

Anyway. Thank fuck for Gumball. I was ready to rock n' roll again. I picked up the phone and called Lucas.

33

Lucas: "Where the fuck have you been?! I've no heard from you in days!"

He wasted no time on small talk.

Me: "I've been partying bro, sorry man. I've got three grams here!"

Lucas: "Bro listen to me. Mikey's fucked up. He's still in hospital."

Me: "Fuck man. What. Wh–"

Lucas: "Have you seen Phil?"

Me: "Phil?"

Lucas: "Aye man where the fuck is he?"

Me: "What do you mean? Did he not leave with youz?"

Lucas: "No he fuckin didnae that's what am telling you!"

Me: "Where the fuck *is* Phil?"

Lucas: "*Stay* there bro. Don't move. I'm diving in a taxi and coming over. Don't go anywhere."

Worry invaded my thoughts. I clenched every face muscle aching for memories to be clearer. Phil was with Scott at RATT. The cinema projectors were playing in my eyeballs again. Them hugging. Arguing. The corridor. I patted my jacket pocket just to make sure it was real. 'Yep, it's still there.' Only one answer.

More cocaine.

I chopped up lines and snorted like a maniac. Rubbing the powder into my gums numbed them to the point my teeth felt like foreign objects in my mouth. My battered face wasn't throbbing anymore. I felt fucking back in my zone. Yet another job was down the shitter and

I couldn't care less. I knew fine well there was worse trouble ahead.

Whilst I waited for Lucas I called Cassie. Well I thought it was her number.

"Hallo," she answered.

God damn that voice.

Me: "Cassie?"

Cassie: "Nathan. Oh my God Nathan why have you been ignoring me?"

Me: "I haven't honestly. My phone was broken but it's fixed now."

Cassie: "How's Mikey? I haven't heard a thing since the rave. We've been so worried!"

Me: "We?"

Cassie: "Me and Erica. She was there too ya know? Mikey was lovely to her. To us both."

I didn't like this at all. It gave me a horrible, sharp feeling in my gut.

Me: "Look I don't want to be the one to do this to you. But I feel it's only fair."

I couldn't believe what I was about to do.

Cassie: "What is it Nathan?"

I fake sighed then carried on.

Me: "Mikey is fucked on opiates alright. He's in a bad way. I really wouldnae recommend being around him now."

Cassie: "Oh."

Me: "I know."

Cassie: "I won't say a word to Erica."

Me: "Ok good. Wait. What?"

Cassie: "I won't tell Erica."

Me: "Aye a heard that. But why would she care?"

I was sniffing like mad, as if I had a cold. Only it was the Columbian cold. Because of the old Peruvian dancing dust.

Cassie: "Are you crazy? The two of them couldn't keep their hands off each other!"

Me: "Wait. Hold on then. So how did you get my number?"

Cassie: "Mikey gave it to me. He told me you liked me. He said you were dealing with some shit that night. But he said you were a great guy. I kinda liked you too, hey. That was, until you went off the radar for days! I thought you were ignoring me."

I felt like a fucking royal cunt just about then.

Lucas was pulling up outside in some shitty taxi.

Me: "Cassie I *reallllly* need to go and sort some shit out just now. But I promise, I fucking promise I will call you back soon."

Cassie: "You better. Cheeky."

Lucas burst through the front door, fag in mouth, wearing blue jeans and a grey trench coat, carrying a sporty black duffle bag. He took one long, hard look at me.

Lucas: "Nathan you fuck!"

After holding the glare we both burst out laughing as he swung his arms around me and hugged me tight, duffel bag flying round the back of me.

Lucas: "Aaaaarrrgggh. Thank fuck you're OK bro! I was fuckin worried about you. Right stick on my song."

As Lucas dove head-first into the coke, I put on 'Operation Blade (Bass in the Place)' by Public Domain.

Zooooopppppp!!! Went a fat line up his beak as he growled.

He snorted line after line like a maniac only stopping to down the Bucky. Once he consumed enough he stopped and wiped his jacket sleeve over his face, his green eyes flickering.

Lucas threw the bag down onto my couch and opened the zipper. Stuck his hand in and pulled out a black, aluminium baseball bat. It had a rubber handle to grip on. I watched on like a wee boy as the bat raised up into the air, Lucas gripping it tight. Green rage danced about in his eyes.

Me: "Aw shit Lucas. What we doing wae that?"

Lucas: "We're gonnae go find Phil!"

CHAPTER 3
GET CATFACE

Chapter Three: Get Catface

"Woooaaah man hold on a fuckin minute!" I said to Lucas as he swung the bat around like a madman.

'Operation Blade' was still pumping.

Me: "Where exactly we goin wae that?"

Lucas: "Where d'you think?!"

Me: "Man it's a fuckin Monday afternoon. Everyone will be at their work."

By now Lucas was swinging me around with him. We were both falling about laughing in hysterics. And there was nothing funny about our predicament.

Lucas: "I'm no giving a fuck! I know fine well those two pricks are behind all of this!"

Me: "What two pricks? Rab n Sunny?"

Lucas: "Well fuckin obviously. What other two cunts d'you know that jumped ye at the weekend like?"

Me: "Aye but what's that got to do wae Phil?"

Lucas: "C'mon tae fuck Nathan. Play the game son. Wake up. Mikey collapses. You get jumped. Phil disappears. Those two are getting it. I won't stop till I know where Phil is!"

Me: "Aye I hear you bro. But it's a bit of a convoluted plot, no?"

Lucas: "How?"

Me: "You think those two dafties jumped me, spiked Mikey *and* abducted Phil? C'mon tae fuck Lucas."

Lucas: "Aye well there is only one way to find out, eh?"

Me: "Right and how are we finding out bro?"

Lucas: "Time to go and see Sunny at his garage. I'll be dragging him out. Right out!"

We were circling each other as we spoke in accelerated exchanges. Like a never-ending spiral of excited rage. High on coke, tipsy on Bucky and pumped the fuck up.

Me: "OK man. OK man. Right. Let's not fly in unprepared though, eh?"

Lucas: "So what you sayin' Nathan?"

Me: "I think we need tae bring someone in on this. Someone they won't suspect."

Lucas came to a halt: "Ahahahaha."

That told me he was game for it. Time to go pick up Catface.

Catface was the biggest weed man in West Lothian. And since Phil was the biggest stoner in town, they knew a lot of the same people. Catface knew everyone. He was only twenty, covered in tattoos, and a trendy wee fucker. If you gave him an instrument he could play it. If you told him an emotion, he could paint it. If you gave him a joint, he would smoke it. You catch my drift. He was a good cunt. No idea why they called him Catface though.

As we left my gaff I noticed Lucas had his Caterpillar boots on. Steel toe caps. He wasn't fucking about like. I kept rubbing my nostrils and breathing in hard. Cocaine ripping through me. The sun was out, and I loved how warm it felt on my face. Between that and the coke buzz I felt like things might just turn out OK after all.

We got in the car and 'Toca Me' by Fragma came on. Lucas revved up and sped off. We were on route to Heatherbank, the street in Ladywell we grew up in. Mikey grew up there too. Catface still lived there.

When we arrived we parked up in the middle of the street, surrounded by a cluster of social housing which had seen better days.

Lucas: "Lots of memories here man."

See Ladywell *was* a violent area to grow up for us, yet we still loved the bones of the place. But we always had this horrible gut feeling following us everywhere. A gut feeling we could only get rid of when we were together. When we got smashed. When we listened to trance. Our lives were high risk but carefree. We lived fast and fuckin well liked it and fuck you if you told us otherwise.

Before I got out of the car to go for Catface, Lucas spoke: "These streets aren't what they used to be, eh bro?"

I nodded. This was the calm before the storm. We both felt it in our gut. As soon as we crossed this line with Sunny, there was no going back.

I jumped out. The sun was still shining down on me. Sometimes I could close my eyes long enough and imagine my grandad giving me a burly bear hug. I needed that right now. But there was no time to get all sentimental.

The stench of grass was waiting there for me at the front door. I made a fist and knocked. The peeling green wood door gently pushed open, and a big waft of potent smoke hit me. That fucking smell man. I peered in.

Me: "Catface?"

I ducked down under a dreamcatcher above the entryway and stepped inside. There were wind chimes hanging from the staircase and an aquarium redesigned into a massive bong. It still had the water in it like. No tropical fish though. I'd walked into another dimension.

I looked around for Bob Marley pictures but there weren't any. Suddenly I caught a sound coming from upstairs. I mean this kind of music wasn't my jam like, but there was another sound too.

It was two cunts arguing. One small step at a time I made my way upstairs. The rapping from the track was getting louder. Something about getting high and taking hits from a bong.

I had a plan: Right, pick up the nearest fucking thing. Dive into the room without warning. Jump the cunt arguing wae Catface. Then we will go and get Sunny. It seemed like a good idea at the time like. I couldn't find a weapon. I spotted the next best thing though: a 'Take a Break' magazine on the floor. I tiptoed over to get it then rolled it into a makeshift weapon. I tightened it and slapped it into the palm of my left hand. 'Good.' That would have to do.

I used the best stealth approach I could as I tiptoed across the hall landing. Smoke rolled out from under the door and the arguing was getting louder. Right. Here goes!

My Adidas gutty morphed into a siege engine, right through the door and I jumped in with a warrior's cry. The sound of my scream met with the sound of... *hers!*

Mine: "Aaaaarrrgghh c'mon ya cunt!"

Hers: "Aaaaaaaaahhhhhhh!"

I looked on in horror to see Catface going to town on this girl doggy style. One joint in his mouth, one resting on his right ear. His eyes were puffy, and he was smiling like a hyena. There were two budgies going fuckin nuts in a cage behind him. He hadn't even noticed me as he kept pounding her. For just a moment she and I became a duet screaming along to the rap track which I now knew was Cypress Hill.

Just as Catface was coming to his climax, Lucas flew into the room swinging the black, aluminium baseball bat.

The girl: "Aaaaaaaaaa!"

Lucas: "Aaaaaaaaaaahhh!"

Me: "Whatttt theeeee fuccckkkkk!"

Lucas turned off the music which brought Catface to a shuddering halt.

He looked at me then back at Catface and the girl.

Lucas: "What the fuck is going on?!"

Me: "I thought this cunt was getting done in."

Catface: "Yo man that was fuckin dope."

The girl scrambled under a purple duvet and grabbed her clothes from the floor as Lucas and I turned our backs, trying to protect her modesty at least.

Lucas pointed the bat over his shoulder at Catface: "That cunt?"

I stood there stunned, surrounded by clouds of smoke.

Me: "Aye. That cunt."

I mean fair play to Catface the girl was tidy, but accidently petrifying her made for an uncomfortable void.

Lucas: "The fuck you reading that magazine for?"

Me: "Naw it's, just... ach never mind."

Catface stuck his CK's on and then his baggy jeans. There was a waiting-room kind of silence between us all now.

Lucas: "You never did tell me. Why the fuck does everyone call you Catface anyway?"

Catface: "Well –"

But before he could answer his date kissed his cheek and raced past us, right down the stairs and out the front door.

We really had no time to waste. So we sat him down and explained the situation. Once we finished, he smiled and nodded.

Catface: "Dope man, you guys know I've got your backs. Lemme just roll a coupla jays."

Lucas: "This place is killing my fuckin buzz man. Nathan get a few fat ones out. You no got any trance in here?"

Catface: "Nah home slice, sorry bro."

He started toking the shit out of that fat J.

Catface: "So, don't youz think Phil is just melted somewhere then?"

Me: "I dunno man. Usually he would at least let Lucas know he was disappearing for a few days. But he has literally said fuck all."

I laid out the charlie on a set of drawers covered with weed grinders and Rizla skins.

Lucas: "Phil always tells me when he's gonnae disappear for a while. *Always*. No cunt has heard from him. He hasn't been seen since RATT. Something isnae right."

Catface: "What about Mikey?"

Lucas: "What about him?"

Catface: "Can you not ask him? See if he's heard anything?"

Lucas: "Mikey's in St John's mate. He's done in. He hasn't been able to stay awake for more than five minutes at a time. His wee brother is camped out at his bedside. And apparently now some bird fae the rave is there."

Me: "That Erica?"

I chopped the coke into three fat, neat lines.

Me: "She must be keen. Only told Cassie an hour ago."

Lucas: "Aye her."

We each proceeded to snort a fat line.

Catface: "Aaah shit man. That's made me feel marshmallowy as fuck."

Suddenly the stoner vibe was gone, and we were wired once again. In the car we discussed how Catface was going to go into the garage with some bullshit chat about a big weed deal to distract Sunny, giving us the chance to blindside him. I must admit it *did* feel like a good plan at the time.

Lucas found a tune that set the tone. Lock N' Load – 'Blow Ya Mind!'

With every sharp bend Lucas took I slid across the back seat with the baseball bat.

Me: "Here we fuckin go!"

Lucas: "Cmmmoooonnn ya cunts!!"

Catface: "Right first things first, you gentlemen know this is a garage aye?"

Lucas and Me: "Aye!"

Catface: "Right. And you gentlemen know this isnae *really* a garage aye?"

Lucas and Me: "AYE!!"

Catface: "Right. Good. Just checking. You know youz are gonna mess up a good weed connection for me now, eh?"

Lucas stared a hole through Catface as he kept one hand steering erratically.

Catface got the point.

Lucas turned the music down low as we pulled up near the garage. We parked up behind a few vans, incognito. The building was down a potholed road at the bottom of a hill, a large, industrial, white-stoned building with a yellow banner at the top with bold black writing: **'Sunny side up'**. Two guys were out front clanking away at what looked like a slump of scrap metal. A skinny rake, and a big lump. It was a shady looking place.

By now 'Fire Wire' by Cosmic Gate was playing. It felt as grungy as I did.

Lucas: "Right man, you know the drill. Nae fucking about. Get that cunt outside. Try get him looking away fae us. Keep him distracted. We'll do the rest."

Catface: "I've got it brethren, no hassles man."

My stomach was a nightmare. Sweat was pishing off my face. I started to inhale heavily, forgetting to exhale. Catface stepped out of the car. He sparked a joint and blazed down towards Sunny's digs.

Lucas: "You ready bro?! Pass the bat."

Our eyes were glued to Catface as he reached the entrance and nodded to the two oddities outside. The oddities nodded back. Catface walked inside the building followed by the skinny rake. Neither of us could sit still. Lucas had the bat hidden up the sleeve of his jacket.

I looked in the rear-view mirror. My face was still mangled up from RATT. Cuts and scrapes everywhere. It reminded me what those animals did to me. I started thinking to myself: 'Fuck Sunny man. He deserves this.'

At least I tried to convince myself he deserved it.

The edge of my seat had my arse going numb. Ready to pounce. Any minute now. Annnny minute now. Waiting.

Lucas: "There he is!"

He ripped open the door and grabbed me by the scruff of my coat and rag dolled me out with him.

'Shit! Be careful!' I was thinking, remembering what was in my fucking coat pocket.

Catface had Sunny deep in conversation, looking the opposite direction from us. Just like we planned. Sunny had oily, blue overalls on. I guess he had to look the part. They were both blazing. We sprinted down the hill, with everything feeling like it was slowing down again.

As we got closer, the big lump started to appear much larger. He saw us and leaped forward like a machine. Sunny spun round in a daze, staggering like a deer about to be smashed by a truck. The big lump pushed Sunny to the side. My legs were filled with jelly.

Lucas slid the bat down into his hand and let out a roar: "Fuckin cmoooon then ya cunntttttt!!!"

He swung heavy, smashing the metal across the big lump's noggin. He dropped to the ground. Sunny threw his arms out wide.

Sunny: "Woooaaah! What the fuck boys?!"

He stumbled backwards into the white brick wall. The skinny wee rake was back out front now. Sleeked out almost unnoticed. He stood to the side of Sunny in a stunned silence. Sunny gave Catface an evil glare. Then he focused on me.

Sunny: "This is your doing ya fuckin dick!"

Lucas shoved the bat into his throat making him gasp.

Lucas: *"Where the fuck is Phil*?!"

He had him pinned to the wall. Sunny's pal just stood staring. Catface kept blazing and slowly walked back to the car.

Lucas: "Where *the fuck* is he?"

Lucas turned demonic pressing the bat in harder.

Sunny: "I have no clue where your idiot cousin is!"

Lucas released the bat from Sunny's throat but Sunny had no time to feel relief. Lucas raised the bat up over his head. Sunny's eyes widened and he hurled his hands up in front of his face.

Sunny: "What the fuck man! I haven't seen Phil! I thought you were here to settle the score for *that* cunt!"

Lucas: "Am gonnae smash your fuckin head in like yer pal there. This is for Mikey too!"

Sunny: "Mikey? What are you talking about ya dobber?!"

In his confusion he dropped his hands.

Sunny: "Why don't you ask that cunt where Mikey gets his little pills fae," again directing his jibes at me.

I was motionless. It was like watching a plane falling from the sky. I couldn't do anything. It might have been a daft move from Sunny. Reminding Lucas of the skull-fucking I took at RATT.

Lucas: "You think you can jump my wee brother as well, eh!"

The bat cut through the air, resulting in a sickening CRACK! Sunny collapsed to the floor gargling in agony to the point I thought I was gonnae spew.

Lucas lifted the bat over his head: "Where is he?!"

Sunny: "I don't know where he is! Ask your brother why we fucking jumped him then. Go on!"

Lucas had heard enough. He aimed the bat at Sunny's head. Sunny waited like a baby lamb for slaughter. Helpless. Maybe that's what made me do what I did next.

Me: "SSTTOOPPP!!!"

I jumped in, bringing everything to a standstill.

Me: "Lucas don't! It was me! It was fuckin me! I've been snorting their gear for months. Taking it all. Any cash I made I spent on more charlie. Fae Gumball. I'm so fuckin sorry man. I know we needed that cash for Phil. I'm so fuckin sorry man. I'm so fuckin sorry!"

I crumpled to my knees. Level with Sunny, who was clutching his legs.

Me: "They didnae fuck us over. *I* fucked *them*."

It felt pathetic. The truth was out.

Lucas didn't say *anything*. I waited and waited but he didn't speak a word. Just stared at me as he exhaled. See the money from the charlie, it was for Phil. We were trying to save his arse. Well save us all really. It's a long story. I'll get to it.

I willed Lucas to say something, but he just stood in disbelief still holding the bat above his head. Then his weaponised arm dropped, as if someone removed his batteries. I had betrayed him. Betrayed them all. My stomach felt like fizz. I shrank into myself. The hole in the ground wouldn't open for me.

The silence eventually broke, but it wasn't Lucas. A van screeched around the corner from the other side of the garage. It was Rab and he had some menacing fuckers with him. That skinny rake must have called him. Lucas just leaned on the bat, still staring at me.

Sunny: "You're done now Lucas! You're fuckin DONE!"

CHAPTER 4

OPERATION PHIL

Chapter Four: Operation Phil

From out of nowhere came burning tyres and the roaring blue Ford Fiesta skidding up beside us. Lucas and I had been so hasty getting to Sunny, we left the keys in the ignition. Like a wasted wizard Catface appeared with the car doors open.Catface: "Let's do one broskis!"

Lucas was still in a daze, so I dragged him into the back of the motor to the sound of Klea – 'Tic Toc (Magik musik remix).' The tunes were ablaze. Speakers and subwoofers at maximum impact as the vocals of the track penetrated us.

Catface threw the gear into reverse and soared backwards as Rab tried to ram us. He manoeuvred around a corner and now we were reversing up the hill. Lucas was starting to come out of the daze as my guts crunched. With the tune still blaring Catface spun the car round, and revved through the gears, catapulting us forward. Rab kept up his pursuit.

As we raced over the middle of a mini roundabout, Lucas looked at me, then at Catface, and asked another very important question.

Lucas: "I thought you didnae like trance?"

Catface toked his fat J, his eyes swollen like little beanbags: "It's growing on me man."

Lucas was molten. I knew I was going to be on the other end of that rage soon. I deserved it. But for now we had Rab ramming us and at best count I could see at least three of their angry mob in the van. Catface flew past traffic lights and roundabouts, the headrests the only thing stopping us from becoming crash test dummies. We looked back to see if we were cutting them loose. But there was no way.

Lucas: "Fuck this! Let's stop."

Me: "Are you off your nut?!"

Lucas: "Take this left. There's a wee industrial estate on the right after that. Pull in there."

Me: "Lucas –"

Lucas: "You fucking better be out there with me bro."

He was gripping the bat, still glistening red from the skull smashing he gave to that big lump. Catface done as instructed and we skidded into the industrial estate with stones and gravel flying around as the death van stayed hot on our tail.

We scrambled out of the car. Catface lit a new joint. Lucas stood in front of us with the bat resting by his side, almost like it was an animal that took instructions from one master only. Rab made haste in approaching us with his mob bundling out of the van. If this was a superhero standoff then Lucas just met his match. Rab held a serrated, steel machete with a brown wooden handle. He raised it right out in front of him as he paced forward.

He stopped inches from us. Gravel crunched below his feet, as he pointed the blade at Lucas.

Rab: "You fucked up pal."

Lucas didn't budge.

Rab: "No one kens where yer fanny of a cousin is. And no one gives a *fuck* about your junkie pal either. But yer wee brother over there owes us nine grand. Sunny's been covering yer arse long enough Nathan. And now you've gone and fucked up big time."

Lucas: "Aye?!"

Rab: "Aye!"

Hearing Rab declare nine grand made my knees buckle. It started off as a cheeky wee gram here and there on the fly. Skimming off what they gave me. A late payment now and then. Adding it to the tick bill. Excuse after excuse. Cunts let me run it up until I was backed into a corner. There was no time to dwell. My t-shirt was soaking under my shirt and jacket. I looked at Catface for a reassuring smile. Still toking.

Rab took a step forward. Lucas mirrored him. My stomach was bubbling. Lucas gripped the bat. Rab's hands shook from gripping the machete. The mob behind him were just waiting to pounce. I could *feel* it from them. Like starved piranhas waiting for a feed.

I knew Lucas could handle himself, but even he couldn't take down all of them. I felt my pocket. I could still feel *that*. The burden I'd been carrying for days. I stepped forward, by my brother's side. Catface stepped forward too.

It was time to open my mouth.

Me: "Rab –"

[In the distance] Wooooooooooo!! Waaaaaaaaaaaa Wooooooooooo!! Waaaaaaaaaaaaa Wooooooooooo!! Waaaaaaaaaaaaa!!

Every fucker there knew fine well what that sound was. Lothian and Borders's finest on the way. What did we expect? Flying around playing car chases on a weekday afternoon in Livi. But before everyone scattered and broke their ranks, Rab turned and pointed his blade right at me.

Rab: "You're a dead man Nathan!"

Lucas didn't take too kindly to that. As a parting gift he swung the bat with fury catching the bridge of Rab's nose. CRACK! It was sickening. Blood spurted as he was pulled back to the van by his mob, shouting all sorts of profanities our way now.

Rab: "This isnae over!"

We sprinted back to the car and clambered in. Lucas took the wheel and Catface lumbered into the back with me and the bat. Without thought he drove over a grassy verge into speeding traffic from both directions. Somehow we got past unscathed. I knew where he was heading. Grandad had owned an old garage of his own. A wee lock up where he used to store vintage cars. Lucas wasted no time.

We pulled up outside. Lucas looked around before he lifted the rusty brown shutter, hopped back in, and drove us into safety. The darkened old lock up smelled of stale biscuits and dead insects. There were spider webs everywhere and half-rotten cardboard boxes filled with obsolete objects. Grandad really did love his useless gadgets. Metal detectors and shit like that.

The darkness was only penetrated by rays of light peeking in through six holes that had been drilled into the brick wall at the back. As Lucas pulled the shutter down and locked us all inside, I let out a sigh of relief.

Me: "Thanks bro –"

BANG!

Fists met face before I could get the rest of my gratitude out. Lucas jumped on me, threw me against the boot of the car and squeezed my throat. I thought my eyes were going to pop out. My air was cut off.

Lucas: "Why didnae you fuckin tell me? Why Nathan? Why?"

He must have asked me about a hundred times. But I couldn't answer with the stranglehold he had on me.

Catface: "This is some bad Juju boys. You forgetting we need tae find Phil?"

Lucas released me. I gasped for air and fell to my knees. With the adrenaline wearing off, I began to sob like a pathetic mess.

Lucas: "How long?"

Me: "Weeks. Months."

Shame completely engulfed me.

Me: "But I don't know where Phil is. I swear to God I don't know."

I sobbed some more, gasping for deep breaths.

Lucas: "I know that bro. I know that. Why didnae you come to me man? We could have sorted it out!"

Me: "Because you have always fucking bailed me out man. Always. I couldn't tell you. I couldn't face Phil."

Lucas: "Listen, I've been bailing you out our whole lives little bro. I'll always bail you out."

59

That set me off even more. We had only gotten into business with Rab and Sunny as a short-term fix. The boys had trusted me to handle it. All along I was snorting the gear and spending whatever cash I made on more gear. Sunny kept giving me time. But I fucked it. We were trying to raise enough cash for Phil to buy a CD back from Scott. Not just any CD.

You see, for a while Scott and Phil were quite the legend all over central Scotland. They were gritty, underground throwbacks to classic rave culture. Their stuff was truly state of the art. Some even said they were bringing us back to the good old days. Everyone thought they were going to make it to dazzling heights. If you could have heard them yourself, you'd get it. Phil was going to take us on the ride with him. Get us out of Livi. Away from the violence we were always getting caught up in. But with each major 'audition' Phil kept fucking up. Like the rest of us he had demons. Gear. It was almost as if it felt too good to be true. As if it felt more comfortable in the world of constant failure. No one expected anything from a failure.

They made two CDs of equal stellar quality, separated only by the patterns on the discs. Scott's was a pattern of red love hearts against a milky white background. Phil's was black intertwined with luminous yellow in a spiral design. The CDs were jam-packed full of their best stuff. Most of it they claimed was new and unheard material.

Scott didn't want to risk anyone hearing his new material and ripping off his style. He'd tested one of his tracks on an audience called 'Acid Hearts' and it blew up.

The discs gained their own lifeforce and mythology. Scott and Phil's reputations started catching fire. Whispers through the grapevine were that they were wanted abroad.

Scott's patience with Phil reached an end. He locked both discs away until Phil sorted his shit out. But Phil couldn't sort his shit out. Scott went solo. Sensei Sounds was born. Scott's rise through the ranks attracted the attention of some heavies who wanted a piece of the action. Now the grapevine was sending out rumours of all sorts of criminal activity going on through Scott's rising enterprise. In fact rumour had it he was in deep with some shady people. Baw deep.

Now Phil couldn't even take back half of what was his. Not unless he wanted to end up wae the trollies in the River Almond. Scott wanted compensation for all of Phil's fuck ups. So Phil would need to buy his disc back. Everyone thought I was storing a nice little package away from the coke deals. But I hoovered the lot. I just couldn't stop myself.

Scott and Phil agreed to meet somewhere neutral, without Scott's goons. When we heard Scott was playing at RATT it made sense to do it there.

As I knelt there in despair it came thundering back again. Both of them belting each other in the rave. The memories had been sliding into my brain in compartmentalized pieces, but a fuller picture was forming.

Catface: "Dude, I hate to ask, but what was Sunny talking about? Y'know, with the pills n shit?"

Me: "Man I fuckin swear to God, it wasn't me. Mikey steals them fae his bird."

Lucas: "His bird hasn't even gone to see him in hospital Nathan. He's lying there comatose, and she doesn't give a fuck. So dinnae get wide. There's no way he's getting it all from her. But dinnae worry I'll be asking him myself once he wakes up."

Lucas paced back and forward muttering the word "fuck".

It felt strange to be in Grandad's old lock up without him here anymore. He had always worried about us boys. Phil and Mikey were the only family we had left. And our mate Snez, but he'd been away for a while. We had a dream. A dream to ride the waves with Phil. To get out of this bittersweet place. But I'd fucked it all up.

That's why, as he paced back and forward, I decided it was time to tell him what I had in my pocket.

Me: "Lucas, I need to show you something."

I pulled myself up and reached into my jacket pocket and took *that* out.

His green eyes shone like the back of a scarab beetle as he stared down into my hands. It was a disc with red love hearts against a milky white background. Protected inside a see-through case.

Lucas: "Ahahahaha! Yes!"

Catface: "Holy shit brother. That's one of the discs, right?"

Lucas: "Not just any disc. Scott's fuckin disc!"

The disc suddenly felt religious, and the moment felt like salvation.

Me: "What the fuck man. Here I've been pure shitting it for days about this Lucas. I'm fucked if Scott finds out."

Lucas: "Naw you're no. Now we have leverage. Where the fuck did you get this?"

Me: "At the rave man. It was just lying there. I barely remember taking it. He must have dropped it."

Lucas: "Who must have dropped it?"

Me: "Scott."

Lucas: "Scott?"

I told them how I'd just had the shit kicked out of me before seeing Phil and Scott going at it. The last thing I remembered was seeing the disc.

Lucas: "We need tae go and see Scott man. But don't say a fuckin word about this. He must know where Phil is."

Catface: "What about those mental gentlemen we just bailed from?"

Lucas: "Fuck those cunts. They will be lying low for a while anyway. We are gonnae need one more favour Catface. Before we try Scott, you need to take us round every stoner gaff in West Lothian. We just need to be sure he isn't melted somewhere first."

Catface: "Operation Phil?"

Lucas: "Operation Phil!"

He didn't need to explain any further. I knew what that look meant. Time to dish up a few more fat ones. Extra fat ones. Aye, I know fine well the irony in it, don't worry.

Lucas: "Stick a track on."

Catface duly obliged and reached into the car. He put on 'Simulated' by Marco V. Holy fuck what a rush. We snorted up fat lines of charlie. Zooooop! Up our greedy beaks. It was time to go looking for Phil once again.

But before that, I needed to give Cassie a bell. I hadn't stopped thinking about her, not even in the middle of all the madness. If anything it made me think about her even more. I told you man. I was in love. I found her intoxicating. I stepped outside with a chilly wind hitting my face.

Cassie: "Hallo," she answered in her sexy, sweet voice.

Me: "Hey, it's me! No update on Mikey yet. He's barely woken up."

Cassie: "Yeh I know. Are you going down to see him?"

Me: "Soon. Just trying to track down my cousin."

Cassie: "Aaah that must have been a crazy night you guys had last Friday, hey?"

Me: "Where are you actually from anyway? Your accent is mental."

Cassie: "South Africa. We moved here when I was young. My accent is Afrikaans."

Me: "I have never heard of Afrikaans in my life! Tell me a word in your language."

Cassie: "Olifant."

Me: "What the fuck is that?"

Cassie: "I'll let you figure it out, hey."

Me: "I'll get back to you on that. So where you stayin then, at your parents bit or you got your own gaff?"

She kindae laughed and sighed at the same time.

Cassie: "No Nathan, I moved here with my aunt, but she passed away when I was young. I don't like talking about it much, OK?"

Me: "Well like, ano we only just met but I feel like we are hitting it off here, know what I mean?"

Cassie: "Yeh, I do too. But I don't want you to judge me."

Me: "For fuck sake Cass I can hardly judge any cunt right now."

Cassie: "My aunt, she died when I was young and that meant leaving me an inheritance behind."

Me: "You lucky fucker! You must be minted!"

Cassie: "Well, hey. But I'd trade it all in a heartbeat for family…"

There was a silence. Fucked if I knew how to break it.

Me: "So… once things calm down a bit, fancy a cheeky wee date then?"

Cassie: "Sure once you come down off that *shut* you are on."

Me: "Shut?"

Cassie: "S-H-I-T!"

Me: "Aaaaah it's that accent again."

Me: "Cass, I know we have only just met, but I swear to God I am going to kick this shit, especially if it gets me a date wae you."

Cassie: "OK, then call me once you do! Oh and I have one more condition."

Me: "Go for it."

Cassie: "You need to try biltong!"

Before I could answer Lucas and Catface emerged. Lucas rapped his fist against a shutter. RATTLE! RATTLE! RATTLE!

Lucas: "Right, enough of this lovey-dovey shit man we need tae go."

Me: "Right Cass, I need tae go. I've nae idea what biltong is."

Cassie: "You'll find out. Cheeky."

She hung up.

Catface stuck Marco V, 'Simulated' back on. I jumped into the back with the bat. Lucas revved up and off we went on our tour of Livi and the outskirts of West Lothian. The mood felt serious now. With each passing hour, we became more concerned about Phil. We could hardly report him missing. We were off our tits and there was far too much heat on us.

One after one we ventured into bohemian gaffs in middle-class estates to grungy dropouts in crack houses. Social schemes to social snobs. Wine bars to beer gardens. Street corners in rough digs to cul-de-sacs in posh hotspots. Catface thought of every cunt who sold green or vallies and even took us to people's work to question them over Phil. No one knew where he was.

After searching for six hours solid, we ended up back in Heatherbank. We dropped Catface back home. Before he left, Lucas wanted to make sure he was going to be OK after the day's events.

Catface: "Man, those cats won't come anywhere near me, not unless they want to lose every good green connection from here tae the Highlands. It's you boys I'm worried about. If you need me again just holler. You know I'm down to clown. Peace out broskis."

Neither of us had an ounce of energy left. It had been a gruelling day. But we had one place left to go. Scott owned a studio in Bathgate. He practically lived in it. We knew we had to go and see him.

Lucas: "Give me the disc man."

I handed it over. He taped it to the bottom of his seat using black masking tape. I swear to God it felt like such a release just to be free of it.

When we arrived, we didn't say anything. Lucas slipped the bat up his right sleeve, and we stepped out of the car. We walked up to the studio with multiple cameras following our every move. A silver Audi TT was parked up like a trophy on show. At a well secured, glass double door, we pressed the buzzer. After what felt like an eternity we were buzzed in.

We walked up a spiral staircase to the second floor where Scott's main studio was. You could tell this place was steeped in money. Everything gleamed, the walls were made from marble and the stairs were fitted with heated carpets. Up on the second floor we ran in to two lumbering goons. They demanded we put our arms out to the side so they could pat us down.

Lucas: "You cunts been watching the movies aye?"

It wasn't long until they discovered the bat and pulled it out from Lucas' sleeve. Just as I worried it was all going to kick off yet again, a steel door opened and Scott stuck his head out. He looked like he hadn't slept since Friday either. His face was twitchy.

Scott: "It's alright gentleman, these boys are here to see me."

Scott spoke in a fake posh accent. The stupid cunt grew up in Howden. He forgets that we knew him back when he popped speckled eccies like the rest of us. Before the money came in and he got the credit to drive about in Audis and wear fancy Rolex watches on tick. All of it just to try and elevate himself in the eyes of other folk. God I hated this prick. He might have been the one who had landed money but at least Phil was *real*.

The studio had karndean laminate flooring which felt expensive on my schemey feet. A long frameless window looked out onto the whole of Bathgate and let the moonlight in. Scott was wearing a silky dressing gown that was far too short for him, stopping at the top of his knees. It was peach and turquoise. His bulky physique stretched the fabric at the shoulders. He was drinking green tea and eating Ferrero Rochets. His face was still twitching like crazy. The corner of his mouth looked like it was hooked on an invisible fishing rod being reeled in for the catch.

Me: "Do all you pretentious pricks get goons like them as part of the package?"

Scott: "Hmmm."

This was a different kind of standoff. He was waiting for us to make the first move. We waited to see who would crack first.

Lucas got tired of it quickly though.

Lucas: "Listen man, where the *fuck* is Phil?"

Scott opened another chocolate. He had vinyl and CDs stacked on shelves, awards in frames, mixing desks, monitors, synths, samplers, computers, workstations, and every piece of technology you could think of. The heavies had pumped a lot of money and investment into smarmy Scott by now.

Scott: "Do you *actually* think for one fucking second, if I knew where that *waster* was, I would be standing here talking to you two idiots?"

Lucas stepped forward, but I grabbed his shoulder.

Scott lifted the cup of green tea to his mouth.

Me: "Your boys out there really checked us over good n' proper Scott. What are they looking for?"

Scott almost choked on the tea. His beady eyes fixed on me over the top of the cup. He *knew* that we knew something about his disc. And we *knew* that he knew. But no one could say a word.

Lucas picked up a picture of Scott and Phil hidden away in the corner. All dusty and forgotten about. It was the two of them at the very beginning. Phil had curtains. Even back then he wore those yellow-tinted shades.

Lucas held the picture up.

Lucas: "Remember this? These were the days when yer music actually meant something ya prick. Before you forgot who you are. Forgot where you came fae! Just tell us where Phil is. We *know* you were the last cunt to see him. Once we know where Phil is, the rest of your problems go away."

Scott: "Listen, *you* better hope that I don't find him before you do."

He didn't follow it up with anything as he was too busy staring past us. Something that caught his attention outside. A roar of laughter erupted.

Scott: "Looks like you boys have other issues."

Lucas and I spun round to see the Fiesta being towed away!

We bolted out of the studio, past the goons, back down the spiral stairs, trying not to fall as we jumped four steps at a time. We raced out onto the street but were too late. Some fucker was towing the car away. Lucas was screaming obscenities into the sky when I noticed my Nokia vibrating in my pocket. It was a text.

"Eleven grand if you want to keep your legs and get the motor back. Sunny."

Fucking hell. That cunt really *did* care more about cash than revenge.

Lucas kept looking up at the sky. Behind us the sound of metal hitting pavement caught our attention as the baseball bat was launched from the second floor. Tossed back to us by the goons. I looked up to see Scott staring down looking plenty pleased with himself.

Lucas retrieved the bat. And then the realisation hit us in an excruciating moment of synchronisation. The fucking disc was in the car!

"Shiiiiiit! Fuck! Fuuuuucckkk!!" we screamed.

The only leverage we had against Scott was taped under the front seat of the Fiesta. The Fiesta which was now being towed away by Sunny's mob.

With both of us brewing, Lucas received a phone call. The timing could have been better like. It was Mikey's wee brother.

Lucas turned to me with the phone still to his ear: "Mikey's awake."

CHAPTER 5
HOME TRUTHS

Chapter Five: Home Truths

"Awwwrrriiiite gadgies!"

Snez winked from his ginger face, which was literally covered in freckles, matched by an overgrown ginger buff on top of his head. It went well with the gold chain and the blue Kappa all-in-one poppers tracksuit. We called him Snez on account of his sickening ability to wipe the floor with everyone at Street Fighter, Super Mario, and pretty much everything else. He jumped out of his boombox of a car to the sound of Cass & Slide – 'Perception (Original Mix).'

Snez: "What's up wae that radge?"

Me: "It's a long story. But thank *fuck* you're here bro. I've missed ye my auld ginger biscuit."

We gave each other a bear hug.

Snez: "I missed you too son."

Me: "You need to take us to St John's man. Mikey just woke up. I'll explain it all on the way."

As Snez drove, Lucas sat brooding in the back. He clutched the bat as if it was the last possession he owned on earth. I filled Snez in on everything. All I could think about was Mikey. I hoped to fuck he was OK. That he didn't wake up brain-dead. Fuck.

Snez: "So I leave you boys for a few weeks and everything goes tae shit?"

Snez wasn't even from Livi, he came from Wester Hailes, then Muirhouse, then no one really knows. But he ended up in Livi barely a teen. He was like our adopted family. His future appeared as bleak as ours. Any whiff at an opportunity for better days always got promptly sniffed out. Maybe that's what bonded us. But for his own reasons he dipped in and out of our lives. We never asked why. We just understood it was his way.

We pulled up outside of St John's, the building lit up against the November night sky.

Snez: "I'll park up boys, youz dive in and gee that shan cunt Mikey a slap and tell him Snez is on the way. That prick will do anything to avoid an arse kicking fae Blanka!"

That's what I loved most about Snez. He made me laugh through all the pain and torment. Still Lucas didnae crack a smile right enough.

Lucas and I made our way inside. I dunno if it was the comedown from the coke, or the time of night, but things felt eerily quiet. The wee hospital shop was in darkness. I could smell latex and alcohol gel and chloramine, which took me right back to my swimming lesson days as a kid. I was a great fucking swimmer by the way. Had all the badges sewn into my trunks and wore them with pride. Did I tell you that already? One of the few things I ever *did* feel proud of in my youth. Anyway, we trudged on through the hospital not saying much, only stopping at a vending machine to pick up a can of Irn Bru and a packet of Skips. Mikey's favourites.

When we arrived at Ward 17, a.k.a. the nut hut, Lucas finally spoke.

Lucas: "I fucking hope he's OK. We need him more than ever."

Me: "Me too bro."

It was a dimly lit ward with very few people about. We found the bay with Mikey's name squiggled up in green marker pen.

As we waltzed in, Erica scurried up from her seat as though apologising to be taking up space.

Lucas: "Nice tae see you again. You're keen, eh?"

We took one look at Mikey in disbelief. He lay there in a flimsy gown with his skin looking like a packet of ham that had been left out for days. Somehow he was still a remarkably good-lookin cunt though.

Erica: "I'll give you a chance to catch up."

She spoke sheepishly through purple lipsticked-lips, with a wee chipmunk voice that matched her little hamster cheeks and petite frame.

Me: "Is Cassie coming by the way?"

Erica: "I'll give her a call. Back in five."

Lucas took one look at Mikey and asked: "So what happened tae yer actual bird then son, she all out of pills?"

Mikey cracked a smile and lifted his middle finger: "Fuck you man!"

We all burst into an awkward laughter. My insides tied in knots once again as I fell into a large wooden seat.

Lucas dragged over a spare plastic chair and placed himself right next to Mikey's face.

Lucas: "So fuckstick, how's the jelly in here?"

Mikey: "It's a bit like the raves man, starts off epic and then ends wae me just lying in here wae an empty tub in my hands."

Me: "Pretty sure you just lie there hawdin yer baws to be fair!"

Lucas: "Aye n it's no our fault you're a lightweight son."

He followed that up with a playful slap to Mikey's forehead.

Mikey played along. The grimace on his face gave him away though. He didnae smell too clever either to be honest.

Mikey: "Fuck you guys."

He pulled himself up and tilted his head back to indicate a question was coming.

Mikey: "Where the fuck is Phil?"

Lucas and I stared at each other with the kind of hopelessness matched only by our comedown from the charlie. He proceeded to fill Mikey in.

Mikey: "What the fuck are you cunts doing here then?!"

In a fury he began ripping hospital drips and bracelets from his body.

Lucas tried to restrain him: "Would you calm the fuck down?"

With a swipe of the arm to swat him away, Mikey accidentally elbowed Lucas in the face. He tore off the last of the hospital wires from his skin, before jumping onto the emerald-green floor. His bare arse hung below a flapping hospital gown.

Mikey: "So Phil's out there somewhere and you cunts are in here fucking about?"

Me: "Fuck you man. We're here to make sure you are awrite and this is the shit we get?"

Before I could get the next sentence out Lucas grabbed Mikey by his gown.

Lucas: "Listen you smug wee fuck, if *you* hadnae been poppin fuckin pills like ye always do, maybe Phil wudnae even be missin."

Confusion took over Mikey's face.

Lucas: "You cannae mind can ye? Stupid cunt! It was me who came with you to the fuckin hospital in an ambulance. Yer lucky to be alive."

Mikey: "Y'know Lucas, I dinnae go casting shit up when you need fuckin bailed out do I? I dinnae give you cunts a hard time for snorting your fairy dust every day."

I jumped up ready to have a go, but Lucas beat me to it, snapping back with venom.

Lucas: "Ahh fuck off ya cunt. If you hadnae been fucked on pills as usual, and *this* cunt wasnae up to his fuckin eyeballs in debt to Sunny then Phil would still be here."

Mikey: "That cuts deep Lucas. Really fucking deep. Wait, what debt?"

Mikey stood there barefoot, looking half-dead, with the gown hanging from his skinny body.

Mikey: "Y'know Lucas, you've always got to act like fucking He-Man, eh? Talking about Phil like he's dead. Giving me shit about pills when we should be out there looking for him."

Me: "He's right Lucas, you cannae just go about smashing every cunt with a bat."

Lucas slowly turned towards me and whispered to himself, "Sunny?"

He looked back at Mikey—who he still gripped by the gown— and this time he *did* ask a question that demanded an answer.

Lucas: "Who gave you the pills at RATT? And don't give me any fucking bullshit."

Me: "Lucas –"

Lucas: "Sssssh."

He hissed: "Was it *this* cunt?"

I may have been his wee brother, but if Lucas thought I gave Mikey the pills I was as good as dead. You see we had this ironic hierarchy of good drugs and bad drugs. Everything up to cocaine was a good drug. Anything close to heroin was frowned upon. We were oblivious hypocrites.

Lucas: "Well, was it?"

Mikey's eyes welled up: "Naw man, naw. It wasn't–"

Lucas: "Bullshit!"

Mikey: "It fuckin wasnae. What else do you want me to say man?"

Lucas let go of Mikey and jumped on me again in a crazed rage. Mikey jumped up onto Lucas's back, almost piggybacking him, the three of us spinning round and crashing into machines and IV drips. You couldn't even tell who was screaming at who anymore as the three of us crashed to the floor. Just as I thought I was going to pass out in a tangled web of hospital chairs and IV drips flapping about like a whip, a glorious ginger ball of energy soared in.

Snez really was a muscly fucker. He pulled Lucas away from us. Mikey stood up, then fell back onto the hospital bed, exhausted. I lay on the floor gasping for air, my already bruised face started to swell. Again.

Snez: "Well this is pure barry intit? Dinnae make me Hadouken all three of you cunts. Youz gonnae behave?"

Snez released his grip on Lucas. As I panted for air I reached up to Mikey.

Me: "Here's your Irn Bru and Skips, Mikey."

By now nurses were peering in to see what the commotion was.

Snez: "Oh aye what's this then?"

He leaned down to pick up a flip phone. It was one of those new ones with the cameras.

Snez: "Who dropped their phone? Lucky youz didnae smash it lads."

A chorus of "not me" replies rang out.

Snez: "So whose fuckin phone is it then?"

Lucas: "Fuckin open it and see!"

Snez: "Ooooooh cheeky haha."

He stuck his tongue out and flipped the phone round to show us. It was Erica posing with that rampant cleavage. It certainly lightened the atmosphere.

Snez: "Nice one Mikey. Nae wonder you've got her in here chokin yer chicken."

Mikey looked fucking furious and scolded him with his eyes.

Me: "Aaah man she was gonnae call Cassie. Geez it. I'll take it down to her. I think she went out for a fag."

As I went to grab it, Snez chucked it over to Lucas to wind Mikey up even more.

Lucas: "Verrry nice, Mikey."

The teasing pissed Mikey off no end.

Lucas: "I can see why you ditched yer bird for her like."

Mikey: "Aww c'mon boys for fuck sake man. Dinnae be dicks gimmee the phone back before she walks in. I really like her, dinnae fuck this up for me."

Lucas raised an eyebrow: "You only fuckin met her on Friday. In fact what is she even doing here anyway?"

Mikey *did* seem overly loved up with someone he just met. But then I could hardly talk. I was bursting at the seams to call Cassie.

As desperate as I was to call her, I was relieved the silly wee game had taken the sting out of the home truths. The relief didn't last long.

Snez: "Gadgie, gadgie, gadgie."

He was scrolling through the pictures pretending to Mikey that he was having a good gander. Mikey was so gullible these days that he fell for it.

Mikey: "I fuckin mean it lads stop –"

Snez kept up the pretence until one of the pictures took a legitimate hold of him. His eyes widened. Regret never looked so obvious.

Me: "What?"

Snez looked up at us all then back at the phone, then back up at us. Still gawking.

Lucas: "Well fuckin spit it out then."

Snez: "Put it this way Mikey, the danger wank I had planned just went right oot the windae."

Lucas was done fucking about and walked over, swiping the phone out of his grasp. All we could see was a reflection of the screen in Lucas's eyes, before he combusted.

Lucas: "You motherfucker!!"

He flew for the exit. Lucky Snez was on hand with his 'Street Fighter grip.' He's just about the only cunt who could hold Lucas back.

Snez: "Use yer heid lad!"

He barely kept Lucas at bay. Veins were bulging from both their foreheads.

Mikey: "What? What? What the fuck is it?"

Me: "What the fuck is going on?"

Lucas catapulted the phone at me: "Fucking look for yourself. That fuckin wee bitch!"

I barely knew the girl, but I couldn't believe what I was seeing. There she was posing with her arms draped around Scott. It felt like witnessing a static crime.

Lucas: "*Tell* me you didnae get the pills from this wee bitch. Just fucking please tell me Mikey."

Mikey: "How do you know that? What did you see in the phone? Let me see!"

I clung to the phone, thinking to myself: Does this mean... Cassie? No. It cannae be. Surely fuckin not.

Lucas: "Mikey, at *what* point did this wee cow give you the fuckin pills man?"

Me: "Scott was in the Aqua room though. It doesn't make sense. Last I saw him, he was rolling about the floor wae Phil."

Mikey: "The fuck has it got to do wae that fanny Scott?"

Me: "THIS!"

I pushed the phone into his face. It felt brutal to break it to him, but it took the heat off me. I'd given Mikey a baggy of coke that night. From the same batch I had been secretly smashing. But I *never* would have given him the pills. I knew they were frying his brain. Now Lucas finally knew the truth. We all did. I was exonerated. Scott was more sinister than any of us realised.

Mikey broke down.

Lucas: "For fuck sake man, what is it with all youz cunts greeting your fucking eyes out?! Where's Catface when you need him."

Snez: "Hey! Am no greetin."

Lucas: "Wait a fuckin minute. We huddled in a wee group at the start of the rave. *You* wanted to follow those two birds into the Moonlight room. I remember now."

Me: "Awww aye! And by the time I found you, youz had changed to another room. Silk. Away from everyone."

The pieces were coming together.

Snez: "Right will some cunt fill in yer old da Snez here. Coz I wasnae fuckin there."

Mikey whined some more. Burst pipe material. The truth came tumbling out. Erica had been seeing Mikey for weeks. Feeding him pills.

Until now, we had put up with Scott causing shit for Phil. Scott was *almost* justified after Phil had damaged their chances so much. But this shit was fucking evil. It was no secret Mikey was hooked on pills. He admitted his bird had ended it with him weeks ago. She'd had enough of his shit.

After his bird bailed and he lost his source of pills, Erica conveniently popped up. We soon realised Scott was the behind it all. Clearly he wanted to weaken the ranks and thought Mikey was the easy target.

Erica would be back any minute. I still couldn't let myself believe Cassie would do this. Surely she wasn't part of it. I couldn't wait any longer. I needed to know.

Me: "Mikey, tell me Cassie isnae involved with this?"

Mikey: "Aww, you mean the lassie you fuckin dobbed me into? Telling her I was fucked on pills Nathan? Here was me trying to hook you up with her and you fucked me over. Some pal you are. Aye mate, she told Erica."

Lucas shook his head at me. Snez did the same, as if I were a wee schoolboy in trouble. I had broken the most important rule of all.

Snez: "Bro code brother, bro code."

Me: "Ach, fuck you Snez."

Mikey "Fuck *you* Nathan."

Lucas "Fuck *you* Mikey."

Snez: "Fuck yez *all*. It's clear to me the first thing we need to do is find Phil. And fuck Phil by the way."

I shrugged my shoulders and shook my head.

Snez: "Well it's not the first time, is it?"

Me: "Nah, *fuck Scott*! He's the cunt behind all of this."

Lucas: "That cunt *must* know where Phil is. We're gonnae have to call him and offer him his disc back. We have no other option."

But we had no disc anymore. We had to fill Mikey in on all of *that* too.

Mikey started to whine again.

Lucas: "Mikey, these fuckin pills have ruined you. You've no backbone anymore. Sort your fuckin shit out. We need to find Phil. Then we all need to get the fuck out of here. We've got one fucking shot at this lads. One fucking chance!"

Those words were electric. Mikey stopped whining and hopped back onto his feet. Snez stopped cracking jokes. Lucas stopped ranting. I stopped panicking. We knew it was time to come back together.

We heard tiny footsteps pitter-patting towards us.

Snez: "Right bawbags, use yer heids."

In a tiny little hurry Erica rushed into the bay.

Erica: "Sorry babes I was literally about to call Cassie when I realised I lost my phone..."

Me: "This phone?"

I held it up, with the screen facing me.

Relief came over her face until I flipped the phone round. Her lips pursed. Pink and red exploded across her face. Snez walked behind her to guard the door in case she wanted to make a run for it. Mikey couldn't bear to look at her.

Lucas: "Give me one fuckin reason why?!"

Erica looked to the floor.

Snez: "C'mon lads, hurry this up, we need to do one."

Lucas handed her the phone: "Call him. Now! Tell him we have his disc and we'll trade it for Phil. Tell him this fucking ends now. No more fucking about."

Erica muttered: "Fine."

After a few flicks of her fingers she placed the phone to her ear. We waited. Then we heard Scott's smarmy voice, muffled.

Erica: "They know."

A small argument went back and forth between them.

Erica: "Well, what do you want me to do about it? Look I did my fuckin best."

She tried speaking in a low voice, as if we weren't all surrounding her listening in.

Eventually Lucas had enough. With one swift movement he slid the bat down his sleeve into his hand.

Erica squealed: "They have your disc!"

She really had the frightened rabbit look now. She might have been an evil cow, but we were hardly going to bash a woman in.

Erica: "They want to trade you for Phil. I know. I know. I *know!*"

We couldn't make out what Scott was saying. We could only pick up on his tone and Erica's vibes. But for the first time, it felt like maybe we had the upper hand here.

Erica: "Ok. Ok I'll tell them. Bye."

She looked up at Lucas, repositioned her stance and pursed her lips.

She had one word to say: "Tiësto!"

That got everyone's attention.

Lucas: "Tiësto it is. Now fuck off!"

His words spat in her face with genuine disgust before he looked over at Snez.

Lucas: "Open the door for this evil little cow, Snez."

Erica ran for it.

Snez: "Catch ye."

Tiësto was coming up a week on Friday. It would take place in a warehouse at Ingliston, where Grandad used to take us all to market. This gave us a bit of time. It would give us all a chance to recover and regroup. For our generation a Tiësto gig was trance in all its glory. The *ultimate* high! There was no better place to get Phil back. It was almost poetic.

Lucas: "Hang tight Phil. Just fucking hang tight."

CHAPTER 6
TIËSTO

Chapter Six: Tiësto

Friday finally came around. This was it. Tiësto. Time to face Scott. Not the Scott we all grew up with. A man now surrounded by people so dangerous even Lucas felt concerned. Though he would never show it. Most importantly, it was time to find Phil.

I turned up at Lucas' house with my carry out in a blue plastic carrier bag. As I walked in the front door, the bottles of Bucky and MD 20/20 clinked away. I was fair chuffed with my blue and white chequered shirt. Especially the thick collar which could be flipped up when wanting to appear that wee bit harder. Seemed every cunt had this shirt now. I didn't care though. It was a belter. My pulling shirt.

I still had high hopes for me and Cassie. Like a shitebag I'd avoided contacting her. She hadn't been in touch with me either. No doubt Erica saw to that. But I knew she would be at Tiësto tonight. Anyone who was anyone would be there.

My neck was fresh with Joop and I had a Silk Cut Smooth resting on my right my ear, with the packet in my shirt pocket on my chest. You could see the purple and silver 'Silk Cut' logo peeking out, just underneath the gold chain I had dangling down. I dinnae smoke, but I knew once the swedgers kicked in later I would need something.

Tunes were blaring: 'Liebe (Trance Mix)' by Ayla. I glanced at my face in the hall mirror. It had cleared up nicely since my skull-fucking at RATT. I could already tell the lines were being chopped up. My intuition was confirmed when I waltzed into a big cloud of smoke in the living room.

Lucas: "Aaaah, awrite shagdog!"

He sprang up to greet me, with Mikey in tow. Each of them gave me a hug, sniffing heavily. Clearly the Peruvian dancing dust was already in their blood stream. My brother's living room table was littered with Stellas, vodka n' Irn Bru, packets of Regals and a CD case covered in glorious white powder.

I wasted no time. Got right down on my knees at the table. I picked up a yellow children's party straw—appropriately cut in half—and snorted a fat line right up my beak. Zoooop! Aaaaah. Fuck me man. Even up there Mikey was twitchy. He cudnae hide the fact that his body still craved the opiates.

Me: "Still on the cold turkey son?"

Mikey gritted his teeth: "Fuck off Nathan. Did you bring the ectos?"

We really did have standards you see. Nae opiates for Mikey, but mountains of charlie and handfuls of eccies, washed down with beer, vodka, Bucky n' Mad Dog. A proper cocktail before Tiësto. And of course, we didn't let the irony of my cocaine problem get in the way. Part of the reason we were in this mess was because of the charlie. Better to ignore that fact. Ignorance is bliss and all that.

Me: "Nah man I thought Snez was bringin them?"

Lucas: "I fuckin told you already Snez was bringing them."

Mikey had that confused look on his face again. Cunt really was forgetting everything these days. Those pills mushed his brain into juice. He just muttered, "Oh aye," as he went for a Stella from the fridge.

I put my hand on Lucas' shoulder.

Me: "Bro what the fuck are we going to do?"

But his reply wasn't what I was looking for.

Lucas: "We are gonnae stick a Tiësto CD on wee bro."

He grinned from ear to ear.

"Awrite gadgies! Ha what's this then? Bat-man and the twins?"

Snez had arrived.

Lucas stood up with the Tiësto track in his grasp. His black bat was leaning against the wall behind him. He picked it up and pointed it at Snez.

Lucas: "Well I'm clearly the bat-man, but where are the twins?" Mikey laughed as it finally clicked: "Awwwwww!"

The stupid prick had the exact same shirt on as me.

Me: "Good one bawbag. Now we're gonnae look like a right pair of dicks!"

Snez flung his arm out with a massive baggy in his palm. Pills of all colours. You'd have thought he just

91

smashed open one of those wee gumball machines. It was more than a bag of pills tae us. It was a bag of self-worth. Confidence.

Snez: "These are Mortal Kombats boys. Strong enough to get you good n proper cunto'd. Got them fae a new source. I had tae trade my pellet gun for this contact, so dig in."

We lunged in, hungry to alter our reality.

I closed my eyes and waited. I heard the sound of 'Traffic!' by Tiësto. Within minutes the tingles came. Starting from the top of my head. Then swimming all the way down my body like the ecstasy was blowing a cool breeze on my skin. The track started to pick up pace. It was building. My head was bobbing. I could feel it on the end of my tongue. The words. They were coming. Aaaah here they came. I had no control anymore. Oh my God the song was peaking. Like an almighty fire the words erupted from my stomach, right up my throat and out of my mouth like sweet heaven!

Me: "I fucking love you boys! Ahahahaha! Yasssss!!!"

Everyone was roaring as the tunes blared. Snez was laughing with pure joy. His face had gone tomato red. Mikey wasn't twitching any more. Lucas smoked and danced with his bat. We huddled in and started jumping up and down, our feet hammering the floorboards.

"Nah nah nah nah, nah nah nah nah, NAH NAH NAH!!" we sang out.

Lucas: "Let's fucking go boys!"

We nipped out front into the chilly Scottish night for a quick smoke before we left. Lucas pulled out a packet of Lambert & Butler and tossed a fag to each of us. Even me!

See I'd always been slagged off for not being a real smoker. Lucas said I didn't inhale properly and always made the tips go all soggy. So no one liked sharing twos with me. I offended their real smokers etiquette. But tonight was special. So I was given the honour of a Lambie Bambie to myself.

We each pressed a fag to our lips. Lucas lit each one of them in a ceremonial fashion. We closed our eyes and sucked in the nicotine. Fuck that felt good, even for a pretend smoker like me. It always did on swedgers to be fair. And I swear it felt like I'd been dreaming of Phil for days leading up to this.

Lucas: "What you thinking about wee bro?"

I exhaled that sweet nicotine into the cold night.

Me: "Rave man. Trance. I'm thinking about the classics. I'm thinking about Synaesthesia by the Thrillseekers!"

Mikey: "Diving Faces, by Liquid Child brer!"

Snez: "Naw gadgies, Children by Robert Miles!"

Me: "If Phil was here he'd be saying Ayla by DJ Taucher."

Sometimes an eccy dunt can catapult you into different emotions. Now we were all poignant.

Me: "What about you bro? What track you thinkin' about?"

Lucas sucked in the last of the nicotine from his fag then pinged it over a neighbour's garden.

Lucas: "Tiësto wee bro. Always Tiësto!"

There was a pause of appreciation.

Lucas: "C'mon fucksticks, let's go and get Phil. Let's bring that daft cunt home."

Snez: "Aye 'mon gadgies, let's dae one!"

We piled into Snez's Volkswagen GTI. It was a shiny metallic green. It matched his outrageous shirt, which I can only describe as a multi-coloured disco ball. He was car daft that boy. When we were kids Snez used to spot BMWs driving past and shout "I tax that car!" Whatever that meant.

Our jaws were swingin by now. He stuck on a Tiësto CD for the journey.

Like a musical defibrillator the sound of 'Suburban Train (Original Mix)' pulled us all back to reality. Suddenly it got very real again. Phil. Scott. We were edging closer.

The first thing that hit me was the freezing autumn air, with a slight shower sprinkling down. Dark skies and ice-cold air always intensified my eccy dunts. Each of us had cherry-red lips from the constant licking and chewing. Waves of electricity danced through my body already as we made our way in.

Once we got inside, we fed on the vibe. The aura. Rumbling vibrations of the tunes pounded through the concrete floor. People were chanting: "Tiësto, Tiësto, Tiësto!" We chanted with them as we slowly approached the main arena. It felt like we were returning to our tribe or something. Between the drugs, the crowd of buzzing sweaty humans, and the fact we were seconds away from seeing Tiësto, it felt like we were inching towards heaven's door.

For lads like us, this was the pinnacle of our existence. Our hopelessness usually fizzed away for just one night at a rave. But to be at a Tiësto gig was on another level. We still had work to do. We knew we were here to face Scott. To finally find our cuz. To bring Phil home. I had no idea what Lucas had up his sleeve. He didn't even have his bat up it. That was left in the GTI with the paraphernalia of our pre-gig cocktail.

Just for a moment, nothing mattered, not Scott or Phil, or what Lucas had planned. We walked into the main arena of the warehouse amongst thousands of other drugged up revellers, pishing with sweat and not giving a single fuck about anything. True ecstasy.

As we clambered in, surrounded by glowsticks and heightened spirituality, there *he* was on a grand stage before us, almost Godlike. Tiësto!!! His name was pulsating in massive white lights behind him. Finally we were here.

The darkness of the warehouse was broken up by flashes of strobe lights, green lasers, red lasers, and mustard coloured smoke, which felt like being wrapped in a cloud of utter fucking joy. The lasers cut through the darkness and attacked our faces like sexy light sabres lighting up our dunts. I caught snapshots of people's faces between flashes of the strobe light.

Tiësto toyed with the crowd. Played a few lesser-known tracks to whet our appetites. I pulled my brother in close to me, kissed his forehead, which by now was already soaked. We kept dancing. Snez lifted Mikey up over his shoulder. Screaming with laughter. It was as close to real happiness as we could get. We just needed Phil back. Then we could feel complete once again.

Glitter and sequins fell from the ceiling. Dropping from a disco ball the size of a wrecking ball. Which also had Tiësto's name in grandiose flashing lights.

"Here we, here we, here we fucking go! The roof, the roof, the roof is on fire! Tiësto, Tiësto, Tiësto!!" the choir of a thousand lost souls suddenly connected as one.

I took one look at my boys. We all mouthed "Holy fuck!!" to each other. 'Adagio for Strings!!' Oh my God. The crowd roared. Glow sticks, strobe lights, whistles, eccied people shoving tongues down each other's throats. People whistled as the beautiful, tragic sound of the track engulfed us. Lucas threw fags at each one of us. We all lit up. Some folk had lighters in the air. The roars continued. A never-ending field of euphoric bodies joined in acclamation. I wanted it to last forever. My shirt was drenched. I hugged my boys so tight it must have bruised them. This was the sweetest darkness I had ever known. It felt like we were home.

As the moshing crowd launched our bodies around like ragdolls I caught a glimpse of Cassie! Holy fuck. She was cramped in at the bar trying to get served. I tried to scream over to the lads but they just laughed back. I twisted Mikey's head in her direction.

Mikey done the 'fancy a pint' hand motion. We made our way over to Cassie. It was no easy task, squeezing past bodies as everyone pushed forward into the mosh. But Mikey kept pushing me from behind and we slowly edged our way towards her. Every few steps I looked back until Snez and Lucas were eventually gone from my view.

96

I'd talk to Cassie, with Mikey as my wingman, then we would go back and find them.

'Adagio for Strings' ended. Tiësto went on to another track to bring the crowd back down a bit before the next peak. I pushed closer to Cassie.

I did my best *Stretch Armstrong* impression to tap Cassie on the shoulder. Her long, shiny bleached hair flowed onto her tanned shoulders. Her earrings reminded me of hula hoops. Cassie spun round and her beautiful face lit up.

Cassie: "Nathan! Mikey!"

Meanwhile Lucas and Snez were swaying back and forth in the sea of ravers. The track was mellow enough for them to hear each other. Their dunt was interrupted when Snez spotted a snakey lookin lad making a beeline right for them. It ripped him from the eccy induced bubble. Lucas cottoned on quickly and came to life too. The snakey lookin lad shoved a note into Snez's chest. It dropped to the floor as he slithered away.

Snez leaned down and retrieved it. Lucas swiftly grabbed it and opened it up.

Lucas: "Phil!"

He grabbed Snez by the scruff of his shirt and dragged him through the crowd.

Snez could barely make out the babbling from Lucas. Tinnitus was in full effect. They were back in the freezing darkness scrambling to the GTI.

Snez: "Wooooaaa, slow down gadgie."

Lucas: "Snez, I know where he is!"

Snez: "Lucas would ye slow down mucker! We should get the others–"

Lucas: "No time Snez. The note says to come alone. I need your car."

Snez: "Fuck that, if you won't wait for the others then I'm coming tae Lucas, nae fuckin aboot now."

Lucas didn't have time to argue. They bolted back to the car. Lucas took the wheel, dropping the keys as he tried to put them in the ignition. Then stalling the car instantly…

Snez: "Slow down gadgie. Use yer heid."

Lucas forced the engine into action. Tyres threw up mud. It was like the dodgems as he avoided parked cars, desperately trying to find a way out. It felt like a maze. After they done a few loops, the entrance turned up. Lucas skelped round corners until they approached a warehouse much like the one they just left behind. Only this one was abandoned in almost complete darkness, lit up by a red glow inside.

They tried to peer in, but couldn't make out anything concrete, leaving them to step into what appeared to be a gloomy tunnel.

Lucas: "Can ye hear that?"

The music got louder, causing Lucas to make haste almost leaving Snez in his trail.

Snez: "Lucas dinnae be a fud, wait up f…"

CLUNK!

Snez: "Rrmmmkkeeeuu!"

THUD!

Lucas: "Snez? …Snez?!"

Nothing.

Lucas looked behind him, but his eyes were met by a thick curtain of black. His own hands hidden from him as he held them in front of his face. Gritty footsteps carried him forward into the unknown. The walls got louder as he moved through with trepidation. It sounded maniacal! To a grungy beat all he could make out was a demonic: *'Ahahahaha... ahahahaha... ahahahaha...'*

Instinct told him to duck as he crept further into the shadows. His hands waved in front of him like dowsing rods, expecting to hit something solid. He wandered. And wandered. His ears doing most of the work. The maniacal laughing tumultuous and more resounding with each step.

Lucas' hands met with a soft slippery material. He realised he was face to face with plastic sheets hanging down, as if they were hooked to something. His eyes started to make out shapes. Chains dubiously hung too. He could barely make out the walls but the dim glow revealed splashes of copper coloured liquid smeared all over the plastic sheets. There was a taste on his tongue like musty damp sawdust.

The wandering was a mentally taxing exercise, pushing sheet after sheet of plastic out of the way as he barged through them, avoiding the chains as best he could. He kept working his way towards the demonic laughing when suddenly he felt a sharp blow to his ribs.

CRACK!

Lucas: "Aaaaaarrrggghh!"

In a second he dropped to one knee. Teeth ground together and fury escaped from his mouth. He couldn't even hear his own reaction to the pain, his senses dulled by the continuous laughing. He knew exactly what time it was. But the bat was back in the car, left behind in the rush. He truly was on his own now.

The crazy laughter became more distorted and disturbing. Lucas shut his eyes to gather his thoughts. Snez was down. He had no bat. He focused on his breathing and took a moment to compose himself.

CRACK! CRACK!

Two brutal blows landed to his left temple. Lucas fell on all fours, barely holding himself up. Blood as thick as honey dripped down his face. The rough floor below cut into his hands and knees. Every breath was a laboured wheeze. Lifting a hand, he grasped in desperation, only finding another plastic sheet.

Lucas' hand slid down the sheet and he tumbled back to the floor. Every breath was like a sword jammed in his lungs. Still the laughing from the track kept on. The grungy beat was now vibrating through his battered body as he slowly dragged himself forward.

'Ahahahaha… ahahahaha… ahahahaha…'

* * *

Mikey and I were now cutting shapes with Cassie and her friends in the crowd. Totally carefree and alive with energy. With the drugs giving me confidence, I danced with her right there in the middle of the best gig of my life. Even though Phil was missing it felt beautiful in the most surreal way. There was something so enchanting about Cassie. She promised me she had no idea Erica had been keeping Mikey sick. She barely knew Scott.

I looked at her pretty face and went for it. It *did* feel like a good idea at the time. I kissed her. She kissed me back. Ya dancer! Something buzzed through my body and it wasn't the eccies or the trance. I pulled Mikey into me like a giddy child and said, "Let's go find the others!"

* * *

'Ahahahaha... ahahahaha... ahahahaha...'

Lucas dragged himself forward, closer to the music. His last bar of energy flashed precariously. If this was a game of *Tekken* he'd need to button bash his way out of it. But this wasn't a game. Staying conscious was his goal. The blood from his head splattered like soup down onto his hands. He clutched at sharp, shallow breaths, sucking in what he could, as his mind kept skipping away from him. Everything fell into autopilot. He crawled until he could go no more and pulled his crippled body into an opening then looked up.

Everything came into view. Techno disco lasers lit up the room, scanning back and forward, with an old-fashioned boombox playing the track on repeat. For the first time, Lucas understood what was going on. He remembered this warehouse like he was last there yesterday. It was like a mini gig with no one else there. Just Lucas and his attackers. Standing before him was a face he was expecting. Scott was holding something in his hands. Lucas lifted his dizzy head, to get a better view. He sat back on one knee and wiped the blood away from his eyes. Lucas muttered the only words that came to mind:

"Fuck you and yer disc, cunt."

BANG! Lucas was smashed in the face once more. Smacked so hard he crashed back into the floor. Boots were all around his face, the hidden figures who had been attacking him still in the guise of darkness.

Grabbing a scruff of his hair, one of the attackers lifted Lucas back up to his knees. He was barely conscious. Blood and sweat dripped from his bloody pulp of a face.

Lucas held onto his mind as much as he could. He realised he was going to have one final say before they finished him off.

Lucas: "Yooouu... don... have a cluuue... dae... you?"

Scott's posture shifted into a more alert one.

Lucas: "You... don... know... where Phil is either."

The goon tightened his grip. Lucas locked eyes with Scott and smiled showing his bloody teeth, proud at his final act of defiance.

Scott stepped forward but it was to Lucas's shock. Scott's eyes were glazed over as he looked again at the object in his hand. By now Lucas could see what it was. A 90s style photograph. A picture of Scott and Phil together. The one from the studio. Scott's face turned to disgust, and his smarmy voice broke the moment.

Scott: "You know who *I* blame for all of this Lucas? Not Phil. I blame you! With me, Phil had a life. He had a chance. We were going to do it together. It was *you* and your fuck whit crew that kept pulling him back. Just know this. Let *this* be your last memory. Phil could have made it big with *me*. But *when* I find him, it's going to end for him the same way it's about to end for you."

Lucas was distracted. Patting his hands over his chest and jeans pockets. Fumbling around under the grasp of the

102

goon holding him until he found what he was searching for. Out came a crushed blue and white packet of Regals. One of the big fuckers shouted to Scott: "Let's end this."

Scott laughed: "Ha! What's wrong Lucas? You want one more draw on the way out? Fucking let him. Let him have his last draw. Then fucking end him."

The goon waiting to strike the final blow had a baseball bat in hand waiting. A shiny chrome bat that would smash through rock with ease. The grip was relinquished.

It took a while for the half-crushed fag to make it to Lucas's lips. Shaky hands and body shivers slowing him down. With great effort he placed a mashed cigarette between the battered flesh of his mouth. The same process repeated as he dug out his lighter.

He knew he was all out of options, so he finished by flicking his bloody fag up at the goon with the bat. His arm felt like dead weight as he swung it towards the goon. The goon watched in amusement as the dead arm fell back to the floor. Scott gave the nod and walked away. The big fucker holding Lucas wrenched his head back as the other goon lifted the bat. Lucas closed his eyes.

'Ahahahaha… ahahahaha… ahahahaha…!'
CRASH! SMASH! RRROOOOOOAAAARR!!

If this was death, it sounded fantastically fucked up. An earthquake of intense smashing surrounded Lucas. He peeked open an eye to find out he indeed wasn't dead. In fact, the demolition included the destruction of the boombox and the music *finally* stopped.

There was a dizzying commotion and chaos filled the room. It eventually subsided, and Lucas could only hear the sound of boots trampling on the ground until they got quieter and more distant.

Tyres screeched from a far-off place. Then footsteps. More footsteps. Getting closer and closer. Lucas was barely holding on. Just as he felt like he had nothing left in the tank, the footsteps rested before him.

Wiping blood from his eyes, the energy bar was at zero. A voiceover should be shouting *GAME OVER* any minute now. But not before Lucas got a gander at who it was.

Lucas: "You?"

Press start to return to the main menu.

Lucas lost consciousness as his body shut down.

CHAPTER 7
4 O'CLOCK
IN THE MORNING

Chapter Seven: 4 o'clock in the morning

'You look like you're in another world
but I can read your mind
It's four o'clock in the morning
and it's starting to get light
now I'm right where I want to be
losing track of time
but I wish that it was still last night'

Lazard – '4 o'clock in the morning' was playing on Cassie's CD player as we drove around in her pink Mini at a similar hour looking for Lucas and Snez. Dark skies were broken up by dashes of white as snow fell like floating ash.

Mikey was in the back, looking ravaged. He was clutching at his hair but much like me, it may well have been from a cinder block of panic. And fear. Suddenly the matching shirts we had on didn't seem that funny. We came to Tiësto to find Phil. Now Lucas and Snez were missing too.

The true weight of guilt was only being held at bay by the uppers still in my system. Cassie looked at me as if to ask, 'Where now?' We had driven round Ingliston in circles for half an hour. It was normal to lose folk in a gig like that, but we couldn't get either of them on their phone. I couldn't shift my horrible gut feeling that something terrible happened. Part of me even secretly suspected Cassie. Surely it was no coincidence, meeting her at the gig and then losing them? But then she *had* just ditched her pals to taxi me and Mikey around everywhere looking for them. I didn't know what to think anymore.

Cassie's washed out eyes now resembling a panda, her mascara having given up the fight during the rave. She still looked beautiful, despite the rave leaving her with wispy damp hair reeking of smoke. We all reeked of smoke. Mikey continued grabbing restlessly at himself, all over his body. He seemed in agony, as if he was mentally disintegrating.

Me: "What's up son?"

In between deep breaths Mikey replied: "Man, it's like having prickly heat crawling up the inside of my skin."

Me: "Cassie pull over somewhere."

Mikey looked flushed. Sweat drenched him and his eyes were sunken and baggy as if the sweat was burrowing tiny holes in his face. With the car slowing down Mikey thrust forward, his head crashing into the back of Cassie's chair.

Mikey: "Aaaaarrggghh!"

Me: "C'mon Mikey, it will pass man. It will pass. I thought you'd been on the cold turkey?"

Mikey: "I lied man. I fuckin lied. I'm sorry man. I can't take it. I just cannae take it!"

Cassie was perplexed. This felt all too familiar to RATT for her. She mouthed to me: What should we do?

With half of my family missing and my best friend withdrawing before my eyes, the honest answer was: "Fuck knows."

Cassie: "Mikey, talk to me. Maybe it will help just to talk? Tell me what it feels like?"

I couldn't tell if Mikey was grinning maniacally or trying to show his displeasure at the gently presented question.

Mikey: "What does it feel like? Well if you take away the fact that my stomach feels like it is being fuckin gutted from the inside out, and my skin feels like it's being grilled alive, that leaves the heid spinning like am on a never-ending carousel. Then there is the internal prickly fuckin heat. I try to keep this shit to myself man, telling anyone makes me want to fold in two. But I'm gonnae get sick real soon. I can feel my bones rubbing together already."

Cassie: "What do you mean Mikey?"

Mikey: "My mind won't stop man. I cannae get it to stop."

Cassie: "Mikey, talk to me, let's help it stop together."

The car was gathering a blanket of snow on the roof. I could feel the chill from outside blending with the car's heating. Cassie was trying her best to soothe Mikey, but she wasn't a street veteran like one of us. For us this was our normal way of life. Though watching the misery devour Mikey was painful to watch, even for me.

Mikey: "Y'know when you fill a sink up with water? Like really fuckin full. Then you pull the plug out. And the water turns into a massive spiral before eventually disappearing down the drain? Well, that's my heid, twenty-four-fuckin-seven. Except the spiral just gets bigger and bigger. Relentless. It's made up of thoughts I cannae control. Brutal fuckin thoughts and they won't leave me alone. And the more I try to ignore them or fight them off, the stronger they get. And just like a spiral they pick up more and more thoughts. But this isnae like the sink. Coz there's nae drainage. Not without the pills. One little pill right now and I get my drainage. And it takes all the pain and sickness with it. That's what it feels like."

Cassie was back to feeling perplexed. The illusion was over. She knew that we were in deep. In the short time that she'd known us it had been a constant conveyor belt of problems. With Mikey lost in his own world, Cassie aimed those eyes in my direction.

Cassie: "Why do you guys do this to yourselves?"

I looked down at the slippery car mat below my feet, as if I was going to find the answers with the wee bit of melting snow on my Rockports. I shrugged. I was usually a heavy bluffer, but I'd run out of gas.

Me: "This is all we have, Cass. We bounce around from one shite job to the next. One shite moment to the next. One failed relationship after the other. What else are we going to do?"

Cassie wasn't having it.

Cassie: "Nathan, all you guys have is a chemical connection. That shut isn't real!"

Me: "Aye Cassie, we know that. But it's as real to us as anything ever has been. That's what people like you will never understand."

Mikey's groans continued. I could barely stomach his withdrawals never mind what that poor cunt must have felt like. At least I still had charlie and swedgers in my system. My comedown was still a few hours away. Then my own war would begin. Mine was more like being a caged animal. But the racing thoughts were already starting.

To make matters worse I was skint. I won't lie, even with my brother and Snez AWOL and Phil no closer to being found, I already started thinking about Gumball. It's an odd fucking thing, but seeing Gumball gave me that same magical feeling I used to get as a child in *Toys "R" Us*. He was always good for tick, even though I owed him hundreds already. Or maybe... Cassie had cash?

Cassie: "Nathan! Would you snap out of it, hey? There's a bloody blizzard on the way, and yo mates are nowhere to be seen."

Something about her Scottish-Afrikaans twang penetrated my fuzzy head. And then there was the track, as if it had predicted this moment:

*'You look like you're in another world
but I can read your mind
It's four o'clock in the morning
and it's starting to get light
now I'm right where I want to be*

losing track of time
but I wish that it was still last night'

Mikey was soaked in sweat now. Ringing like a dank dish cloth. His hair was matted and his face grubby, like he just popped up from a shift in a coal mine. But he still had some wits about him.

Mikey: "Nathan, where was that fuckin warehouse we all used to go to? Scott and Phil. They used to take us there. Our own personal wee gigs."

His words invaded my brain the way a glorious rave track does when you first hear it. Memories flooded back without invitation and just for a moment I closed my eyes and travelled back in time.

Scott and Phil man. They had dreams. Those wee pretend gigs meant everything to us back then. Of course Phil knew Ingliston well. Grandad took us all to market as kids. I could still feel the heat emanating from my six-pack of sugary mini doughnuts that Grandad would buy as we wandered around the marketplace. A place teeming with life. Meat vans and butchers with white aprons stained orange with blood, and white trilby hats haggled through loudspeakers. Clothes racks with hooky gear sold at cheap prices. Stalls with the latest pirated VHS tapes and Amiga games. Sega Mega Drive and Super Nintendo games. Wrestling figures and Action Men. All of it on the cheap. No questions asked about where they came from. The whole place had such a buzz to it.

Phil found an abandoned warehouse one time and told us it was perfect. It'd been closed for years.

Unoccupied. We guessed it must have been a biscuit factory. Scott always had a bit of cash and had this wee boombox that played tapes. Him and Phil would make cassette tapes and we would go to the warehouse for hours at a time. It was the most freedom any of us ever knew. Scott and Phil were in their element.

Me: "Holy fuck. Cass, I know where they are!"

We sped through the blizzard and raced towards the old warehouse.

Mikey was lying flat on the backseats like a dying hospital patient. My eyes burned with nostalgia. We were getting closer. I was fuelled by adrenaline and eccies as the warehouse came into view. There she was. Still standing, concealing our precious memories and keeping them safe. The old girl had seen better days. Graffiti everywhere and wooden panel covered windows. It was like visiting a distant family member. It felt eerily silent. The snow was coming down rapid restricting our view.

Cassie: "Hey there's a car over there! A green GTI."

Me: "Snez!

Cassie slammed the breaks. Her car near enough did a 360 but I wasted no time in jumping out, spinning round until I fell on my knees. I dragged myself in the direction of the car, the snow slowing me down. Looking back, Cassie and Mikey were out of sight. I pulled on the handle, forcing it open with every bit of eccy strength I had. Grabbing onto the car roof, I steadied myself and looked in.

Me: "Snez!"

"Aaaah, gaaaadddgggie," Snez said with a sandy throat. Dried blood camouflaged his ginger face. Lucas wasn't there. Even more worrying, his bat was. It just lay on the backseat.

Me: "What the fuck happened?"

I crawled in beside Snez, gently lifting his head and hugging him tight. Every time it felt like we were closer to Phil another one of my brothers was getting hurt. It felt like *Groundhog Day*.

Me: "Where's Lucas?"

Snez took a laboured breath: "A dunno gadgie. A dunno. A tried to Dhalsim the cunts, but they blindsided me. Lucas was already away in."

Me: "Fuck! Wait here Snez —"

Snez: "I've already checked in there ya fud. He's no there man. And some cunt took ma gear and ma keys as well."

I realised it was totally down to me now. Everyone I loved was missing or wounded in action. Like the sky had fallen in on us. There was only one short term solution. We needed gear. Lots of gear. I knew my next question for Snez was futile but I asked anyway.

Me: "Phil?"

Snez shook his head.

Me: "Right son, we need tae get out of here."

I rapped my fist into the horn a few times to alert Cassie then grabbed the bat from the backseat and hauled Snez out of the car.

BEEP BEEP BEEP BEEP!!!!

We hobbled towards the sound of the car horn. Beams from headlights cut through the snow and we dove

114

into Cassie's pink Mini. Snez bundled into the back with Mikey. It was like a makeshift hospital ward back there.

Cassie: "I take it you're Snez then?"

Snez: "The very one."

Cassie looked at me: "Your brother?"

I shook my head. I didn't want to ask her what came out of my mouth next.

Me: "Cass, can you lend me some cash. About, like two hunner quid, I'll pay you back next week, I promise."

I had no way of paying her back. I had no job anymore. But I needed coke. I was getting restless. Agitated. Mikey needed anything opiate-based and Snez needed eccies. We needed a fucking cocktail of epic proportions. Big enough to make even the *Happy Mondays* twist their melons. Base was top of the list for everyone. Gumball would tick me but for that motherload of drugs I would need to pay something upfront at least.

Cassie sighed. I wondered if that was the moment where she realised I was a waste of space and that somehow she was already involved with me. But she agreed. And that's all that mattered if I'm completely straight with you. I was in no way game for a comedown.

One quick phone call to Gumball would sort us out. There were always shite dealers who cut their gear and would text at 1am to announce, 'SHOP CLOSED.' This would piss Lucas off no end. He would always rant at these texts saying, "What kind of fuckin drug dealer shuts shop when you need a hit most? Cunts!" I had to agree with him there. We always had to play by their rules. One of our dealers disguised his drop offs by delivering chippies. Had to order a fucking bag of chips every time we wanted a few grams. 'Salt n vinegar on the chips please and a bag of pure.'

Gumball was predictable and reliable. He loved the easy cash and loved a good tick bill even more.

Gumball: "Aye nae bother mate, what ye after?"

I could tell his dick was getting hard down the phone when I told him how much gear we needed. Jackpot for Gumball. The cunt. Reliable cunt though.

The effect was truly amazing when I told the boys that drugs were on the way. Suddenly Snez and Mikey were celebrating as if we had won the fucking lottery. Excitement filled the air and happiness found its way back to us as Cassie, now tired and traumatised from the evening's shenanigans, drove us to pick up our bag of goodies.

If you think it's only kids that ask "Are we there yet? Are we there yet?" then you've never been on a car journey at 4 o'clock in the morning with drug-hungry lads on the way to score gear. I was in and out of Gumball's house quicker than a firefighter saving babies. I returned to the motor with a perfect assortment. Base, opiates, charlie, swedgers.

Mikey went straight for the opiates, before taking a bash of them all. Snez gubbed his eccies followed by the rest of the uppers. I snorted a big fat line of charlie, followed by the rest of the uppers.

We were high as fuck again. Right on the edge of reality where our comfort zone existed. I navigated the control system. The car's CD player that is. It was an otherworldly experience and if there was ever a better sound to hear at that moment I can't imagine it.

'Mesdames, messieurs
Le disc-jockey Sash! est de retour
Encore une fois
Encore une fois!'

Fucking elation! The shellshocked Cassie was left to wonder how three lads who were missing two people they loved most could be so exuberant that they shook her car from side to side, in the middle of a blizzard, not long past 4 o'clock in the morning. Welcome to the irony of lad culture. At least Phil told me that's what they were calling it in the media. Cunts. Fuck them all. They'll never understand what it's like to be us.

I was so high my eyeballs felt like they were in communion with everyone else's eyeballs. Mikey and Snez were so high they had turned to face each other, noses touching as they expressed their love for one another.

Snez: "I fucking love you Mikey. We're gonnae find Lucas and Phil man."

Mikey: "Aye man. I know man. I feel the same mate. I really love you mate."

By now they were as close as those two cartoon dogs in *Lady and the Tramp*.

Snez: "Mucker I mean it man. I fucking love you."

Me: "Cassie, I fuckin love *you*—Cassie shook her head—This isnae the drugs speaking. I mean I know it's been a bit mental and that man. Like this is the last fuckin time I take drugs honestly. From Monday am gonnae get a new job. I'm leaving this all behind."

Encore une fois
Encore une fois!

Cassie had her head in her hands now, resting on her steering wheel in disbelief, still sitting outside Gumball's house with the snow howling down.

Mikey: "Aye Nathan man get me a job tae man. We should see if we can get shares man. We can build it up man. Lead us to the big time."

Snez was now laughing in hysterics. Uncontrollably. Which set Mikey off too.

Snez: "Ahahaha what you talking about man?"

Mikey: "I dunno man. I don't even know why I said that. Ahahaha."

Snez: "But I fuckin do love you bro. I know I'm not always here but I'm never not here."

Mikey nodded with a deep philosophical understanding of the moment.

Snez: "One more time!"

Mikey: "What?"

Snez: "That's what it means. Encore une fois. One more time."

Mikey: "Naw it duznae. It means once again."

Snez pushed his face harder into Mikey's: "It fuckin means one more time!"

Mikey: "Once again!!!!"

Snez: "One more time!!!!"

Snez grabbed Mikey's shirt and Mikey returned the favour.

118

I turned to Cassie who now looked like she had lost the will to live.

Me: "Hey Cass, what does oliphant mean anyway?"

Cassie: "Elephant, you dumb arse. What are we going to do now? Where am I taking you?"

Cassie: "You guys know they practically both mean the same thing?"

As quick as the click of a finger, Snez and Mikey were pals again. The tone of their conversation altered once more. In fact the conversation took a weird twist.

With their noses still glued together Mikey had another philosophical moment.

Mikey: "We are shepherds man. Fuck. I just realised in this very moment that we are all shepherds. All of us in this car."

Snez: "Gadgie, we are! We are shepherds, man. We are fucking shepherds."

Me: "Shepherds?"

Mikey: "Aye man, like there is a reason for all of this. It's our destiny to bring Phil and Lucas home. Like shepherds!"

Mikey's face lit up. He couldn't contain himself. Cassie was still searching for words and my face was still searching for expressions.

Snez: "Aaah it's barry like. I cannae believe it. All this time I knew youz were my brothers. But now you are my shepherd brothers."

I don't know if it was an eccy dunt but suddenly out of nowhere, with no explanation whatsoever, I realised I was a shepherd too. I *needed* to tell Cassie.

Me: "Holy fuck Cass, I'm a shepherd too. It all makes sense now."

Cassie: "Aaaaaaaaaggghhhh!"

Me: "Wassuuppp Cassssiiie?"

THUD!!!

Cassie: "Aaaaaaaaaggghhhh!"

Mikey: "Holy fuckin shit, who are they?"

There are times when something so serious occurs that it sobers you up instantly and snaps you out of whatever gouch you're in. This was one of those times. The drug trip was over. Cassie had turned the music off to scream for our attention but none of us had noticed. But we fucking well noticed now. Her pink Mini was cordoned off by three white vans, and surrounded by men donned in black, wearing balaclavas.

They must have been to B&Q because they had every type of fucking weapon you could imagine. That thudding sound was an axe going into Cassie's bonnet, where it was now planted, the wooden end sticking up. They swarmed us. There was no way out. Sledgehammers, hammers, fuck one guy even had a pair of sheers, I swear it.

One by one they started smashing into Cassie's car as her screams filled the air, accompanied by Snez and Mikey taking turns to shout, "Oh shit, oh shit!" Whilst my fear resulted in widening eyes and a sudden silence.

They took out her wing mirrors first. SMASH! Followed by her headlights and break lights. In came the back window as Snez and Mikey ducked down, being rained upon by tiny shards of razor-sharp glass. We were too terrified to move.

The mob were relentless and merciless, taking out the side windows as we all got pelted with glass. Cassie was shaking so hard I worried she was going to hurt herself. To make matters worse the snow invaded the car through the shattered windows.

A cacophony of growls and groans could be heard as they caved in the front windscreen with the swing of a sledgehammer. The cunts even ripped off the massive eyelashes Cassie had on her headlights. 'Holy shit, holy shit, we're gonna die, we're gonna die' was all I could think.

Snez was gripping Lucas' bat but it was fucking futile man. He wouldn't even get one swing of it without having his head caved in. I turned to look at Mikey as the smashing stopped. Suddenly the car dropped as the tyres were slashed too. Cassie stared into her steering wheel and wouldn't look up. One of the men removed his mask.

Rab!

He cocked his head to the side, gutting my soul with those eyes. Without saying a word he took two steps back and opened the rear end of the van. Out came Sunny.

He limped out of the van with a walking cane. The memory of Lucas smashing his legs in at the garage still strong in my psyche.

Chewing his gum furiously, he approached the car. His cane sliced into the snow with each crunchy footstep. The car looked like a spent grenade as Sunny stood before us.

Sunny: "You lost someone?"

His tone was full of disgust, but he couldn't stop smiling. His moment had come.

Mikey: "Man just tell us if you have Phil. Please man. We can sort all of this out."

Rab stood next to Sunny, with their mob still surrounding us.

Rab: "This Scott cunt, youz clearly have something he wants."

Sunny: "Aye it certainly seems this Scott character is making waves."

Sunny leaned on Rab, stroked his chin with his hand, then rested back onto his cane. By now we were freezing and fraught with nerves. Their adrenaline pumped.

Rab: "Scott's a very well-connected guy, eh? And you boys are in deep. You're gonnae be our bait. Cunts."

Sunny: "Whatever it is he wants, you better bring it to Rezerection next week. You tell that dobber you have whatever it is that's made him to go these lengths. And tell him to bring cash."

Sunny tapped the cane against the car, "You owe me!"

He slowly turned to walk away through the snowstorm, as we all cowered in fear.

Sunny: "And by owing me, I mean for this."

He clicked his fingers. Three of his mob dragged a half-conscious, bandaged up Lucas from behind a van.

"LUCAS!" we screamed, each of us forgetting our fear and diving out of the car. Well apart from Cassie. She didn't budge. The mob threw Lucas and he fell into us.

Lucas, with his head bobbing, looked up at me.

Lucas: "Alright boys, took ye so long?"

Sunny, Rab, and their mob piled into the vans, giving one final declaration as we stood watching with the blizzard still upon us.

"Rezerection!"

CHAPTER 8
FADE TO GREY

Chapter Eight: Fade To Grey

We burst through the doors of A&E despite Lucas protesting, "No fuckin hospitals!"

He could barely stand as Mikey and Snez hauled him in whilst Cassie and I raced up to the front desk to declare that this was a real emergency. Lucas dropped to the floor and started convulsing. Mikey and Snez tried to pin down his arms and legs to stop him from hurting himself any further. I rushed over and held his head, which was thrashing about.

We started as an obvious burden to the staff who'd been giving us disapproving looks. But now the cunts were taking us seriously. Nurses and other medical staff bolted through to the waiting area to tend to Lucas. They called for help and the scene got blurry and chaotic. We were told to get back as they strapped him into a gurney. Not again. Fucking hell not again. Mikey was having flashbacks.

We tried to follow them through but were abruptly told that only one person could go in. Mikey decided to be that person. I reckon he felt he owed it to Lucas. Roles reversed.

Snez stayed with me and Cassie in the waiting area. I think that's when everything hit Cassie. She sat with her head in her hands.

Me: "Cass, are you alright?"

Cassie: "No I'm fucking not, hey. Your brother… And my car!"

Snez: "Aye that's a shan one that pal."

He looked over at me.

Snez: "You awrite mucker?"

Me: "Nah man. We're out of our depth here brother. Without Lucas."

Nothing else needed saying.

We couldn't move. That atmosphere in the waiting area felt haunted. I must have gone up to that desk a hundred times looking for an update only to be rebuffed. To make matters worse, the comedown came in force. Snez was gripping the plastic chair he was sitting on. I was pacing. I made regular trips to the water fountain to get rid of the cotton mouth.

Cassie: "Are you OK?"

Me: "I can't lose him Cass, I just cannae lose him!"

Snez: "Dinnae speak like that mucker."

I couldn't help it. Without Lucas I just didn't know how to survive in this world.

What felt like days was actually around five hours when a doctor finally came through to speak to us.

Serious Doctor: "I'm afraid that your brother is refusing our advice to stay in overnight for observations.

Realistically he should be staying in for at least a few days –"

Me: "Fuck Doc, so he is OK then?!"

Serious Doctor: "Well, he is lucky to be alive, but I wouldn't go as far as OK. He has serious concussion, some internal bleeding and a few broken ribs. At this stage he really should be under hourly observations. Head injuries like this can lead to a coma but he is refusing to stay. Might one of you have a word with him?"

Me: "Fuck Doc, he won't listen to any of us!"

Serious Doc: "Very well then. My advice to you is to check in on him every hour. The next twelve hours are going to be critical. He'll be on some pretty serious doses of medication. I'm afraid the next few weeks aren't going to be pretty. Any issues bring him back immediately."

After a while a stitched up and medicated Lucas came out clutching a bottle of painkillers, leaning on Mikey for support.

We agreed in that moment that we all needed to stick together and camp out with Lucas at his house until the Rez rave. Cassie understandably bailed to go sort out her car problems. No number of apologies from me washed. I think I'd truly gone and fucked it now.

We got Lucas home and tucked into his bed. I laid his baseball bat up against the wall. Lucas was soon deep-snoring due to the combination of strong meds. It scared me to see him this way. We set a timer on a wee digital watch. Twelve hours started now. Truth be told, we checked in on him twice an hour if not more.

Six hours in and he was still breathing, in a heavy slumber.

Eight hours in and he was still OK.

Nine hours in and Snez was doing a check.

Snez: "Gadgies!!! Fuckin gadgies!!"

That guttural scream didn't sound right. Mikey and I had fallen asleep on the couches and awoke to Snez screaming. We ran through as fast as we could!

Lucas was unresponsive. We shook him and shook him. He was as stiff as a dead cat on the side of the road.

Me: "Oh my fuckin God, he's gone. He's gone!"

Mikey: "Lucas wake up you stupid bastard!"

The three of us shook him so hard he nearly fell out the bed. I'd stopped breathing. I was holding my breath without realising. Suddenly Lucas started to moan and wriggle, and I finally exhaled.

He murmured incoherently.

Lucas: "Don't trust them boys. Don't trust 'em."

Then he slumped back into a heavy slumber. The three of us looked at each other. Just stood there in silence. That shook us all the fuck up. Everything felt bleak.

Snez, Mikey and I agreed we needed to crack some tunes on so we started up the PC in the living room. Snez pulled out a wee treat he'd be saving for a special occasion. A mammoth joint. Now weed wasn't exactly my drug but I needed a downer right about then. My nerves were shot.

Me: "You sneaky cunt! Where did that come from?"

Snez: "Been saving it for a special occasion lads, but now seems like a gid time."

Mikey: "Fuckin right it is, spark it up."

Snez: "First, let's stick the right tune on muckers."

Mikey dug around looking for CDs and found Visage – 'Fade To Grey.'

Phil always said these type of tracks gave birth to trance.

I was thinking I hoped it would also resurrect Lucas.

We took turns sucking on the fat doobie. I couldn't help thinking that our whole lives were fading to grey. Every time the raves were over, we faded back to grey. Right now *everything* was fading to grey.

We finally hit the twelve-hour mark. We checked in on Lucas. Still breathing. Thank fuck. We thought we might be out of the woods. We camped back out in the living room listening to tunes. Mikey put on 'Castles in the Sky' by Ian Van Dahl. Something about the track opened us all up. Snez lit the rest of the fat joint we'd been nursing.

Me: "Snez, can I ask something bro?"

Snez raised his eyebrows and nodded, as he kept toking the arse end of the spliff.

Me: "Mind when we were kids, and you would shout 'tax that car' at supercars when they drove past. What exactly did that mean?"

The answer came from Mikey though.

Mikey: "Simple man. It's coz he knew he would never have a car like that in his life. We all knew it."

Snez didn't say anything.

I turned to face Mikey and raised my eyebrows, asking him to expand on his point.

Mikey: "It's Castles in the Sky man."

Me: "What?"

Mikey: "Think about the lyrics man. Like it asks why we are buildin castles in the sky. And why those fuckin castles are up high. It's our dreams and hopes man. Unreachable. Maybe it's why we have nae qualifications. Nae careers. And the only house we have between us is the one yer granny n grandad left behind. Maybe it's all just Castles in the Sky."

The track came to an end.

Me: "Ye know, I remember when Lucas got that bat."

Mikey: "Was it no yer grandad that got him it?"

Me: "Aye man, at Ingliston market."

Mikey: "That's right man, when we were having issues with the lads from Knightstridge and Craigshill."

Snez: "Aaah the gid old wars between LYT, Crazy Hill, and K'TOI."

Mikey: "We were just wee bairns back then tae."

Another Lucas memory was triggered for me.

Me: "Youz mind that time in Club Earth where he gave that lassie a fake name and she was telling all her pals?"

We all burst out laughing.

Mikey: "Aye she told everyone she was pulling Ebeneezer Goode."

Snez: "Ahahaha class gadgie. Class!"

Just then we heard what sounded like Lucas throwing up his guts. We ran through, and he was spewing up blood and bile. I ran back to get a basin and put it under his face to catch the blood.

The next few days were more of the same. After a few days the stitches were out but he was still on the meds which knocked him out cold. His memory was shot to fuck.

* * *

Lucas shot upright in a cold sweat. He felt like his skull was being ripped out of his head. He started to peel off soggy bandages that reeked of puss and blood. He was groggy and slowly coming to. Then it all came back to him. He remembered what Sunny told Rab in the van. He heard them talking in between phases of unconsciousness. Raising his right hand he felt where the stitches had been in his head. It was still alien to touch, like someone had sewn a burst leather football back together. He looked all around to gather his bearings. He was in his own room. The *Monkey Island* poster on his sky-blue bedroom wall told him that much.

He clenched every face muscle as he tried to pull himself out of bed, only tumbling to the floor and eating carpet. His body felt as frail as a spindly tree. But he couldn't chance it. He had to get up and tell the lads. But before he could, he was out like a light again.

CHAPTER 9

SONIC BOOM

Chapter Nine: Sonic Boom

DJ Rankin was in the mix, motherfucker!

And just like that it was the day of Rezerection and we were back on it. Happy hardcore tunes blaring. Fuck knows how Lucas slept through it. The bass alone vibrated through the walls. Every now and then a little piece of peeling wallpaper would crumble to the floor like fag ash. It didn't feel the same as a normal sesh. The three of us were dancing around, but we just couldn't get any traction on a dunt.

The stench of weed hung in the air. Jaws swinging. Space hopper eyes. MD 20/20, White Lightning, Bucky. Regals and Silk Cuts lit. Lynx Africa under the armpits. Joop splashed on the neck. Nae matching shirts for me and Mikey this time. A crisp white Ben Sherman number for me. Plain black for Mikey, but with grey rims on his collar and cuffs. Snez borrowed one of Lucas's short sleeved shirts. Light blue. Not his usual get up. The last of our cash was spent on the carry out of booze and cocktail of drugs—cheers Gumball.

I put on 'Elements' by Neo Cortex to tease my dunt into showing up.

This was it. One last check on Lucas before going off into the unknown. He was still chewing on his pillow in a deep slumber. I left a fresh glass of water at his bedside table.

Thank fuck Snez got the trusty GTI back. It was gonnae feel empty in there just the three of us. As we stood in a triangle, inhaling joints, fags, and the track, I pulled something out for Snez. Something he had long forgotten about.

Snez: "Aaaaah gadgie. Hahaha. That was a long time ago mucker."

I smiled at him and felt pure love for my boys. My family. And not because of the eccies. You see in our world there were three types of people:

Acquaintances: who you bonded with purely over drugs. When drugs weren't in the equation, the acquaintances were absent. Whether you used together, bought, or sold to one another, or hooked a brother up with a dealer, that was the extent of the acquaintance.

Then there was family: aunties, uncles, cousins and liquorish all sorts that you never heard from, but maybe one or two cherished souls like Grandad.

And then there were your friends: they were your real family. Your authentic family. Bloodlines didn't matter. Growing up how we did, meant your friends were fucking everything.

I'd handed Snez the strip of paper we'd torn off the front of a White Lightning bottle when we were fourteen. On the back we'd written – 'Snez and Nathan, cider pissheads forever.' We'd signed and dated it. Stuff like that meant more to me than anything else.

Snez began to breath erratically. Just came out of nowhere. He couldn't control it. I knew we were all feeling it, but it took me and Mikey by surprise.

Mikey: "C'mon man it's gonnae be OK. Honestly. We're gonnae be fine. Lucas is gonnae be fine too. Dinnae panic, Snez."

As Mikey's words rang untrue, with all of us knowing there was no way out, that we were like three lads on death row just waiting to have our names called, we pulled Snez into a three-way bearhug until his breathing finally slowed down. Not a morsel of hope between us.

Then it was time for the gig. Though we'd hardly be raving. The thought of Sunny, Rab... and Scott thrown into the mix, was an early comedown waiting to be had.

The icy air assaulted my face as soon as I stepped outside, bottle in hand. Snez stood in the alleyway in front of the house, shivering in the freezing cold, watching snow fall from fat clouds. Each breath he exhaled looked like steam evaporating from his body. I nudged him with a shoulder barge.

Me: "Oi bawbag!"

Snez shook his head as if coming back to life. The drugs feast really was meagre on account of the near bankrupt state we were in.

Snez: "I love you mate. You've always been there for me ya mad radge. Out of everyone I've ever known, you have always had my back the most. Dinnae ever forget it mucker."

Before I could say anything, Mikey came outside carrying three overcoats.

Mikey: "Right lads, lets fucking do this. Lucas is sound asleep. It's time to go."

The three of us jumped into the GTI. I sat in the back. It felt really lonely back there without Lucas and his bat. The mood was all wrong. The vibe was low. Usually the uppers would have us at Mach 10 speed. The death row feeling was gone. Now it felt more like being driven to a crematorium.

Before long we made it to Rezerection. The atmosphere as raw and alive as ever. I was jealous of the carefree souls surrounding us. Crowds of them diving into the gaudy trance tents. Our usual schemey raver prowess had been tamed. So we just went straight inside.

Our movements were slow and laboured. The eccy dunt wasn't hitting us properly. It was as if it just didn't work anymore. The feelings of invincibility were absent. All the same people were there — whistles and glowsticks galore, flashing lights, epic tunes and rumbling, filthy alcohol-soaked floors, familiar smoky smells, people drugged out of their tits — but the spark was missing. We couldn't even fake it.

We twitched and glitched. Looked over our shoulders and sometimes spun right around thinking someone was going to jump us from behind like animals that know they are being hunted. We barely spoke a word to each other.

We moved through the crowd of loved up humans and tried to find a safe spot in the middle. It felt like the comedown had arrived before the high. I was blinking on a loop to keep my heavy eyelids open and dragging my sandbag of a body. I looked at Mikey and cracked a smile packed with false optimism. He returned the gesture. That's when it came on. A glorious fucking track, Ralph Fridge – 'Angel.'

The robotic, space-like opening set up the intensity of the moment. Followed by a melodic, operatic chanting, which felt like an angel literally swam into my soul and set a bomb off inside the core of my senses. Tingles soared through my body making me feel higher than high, more than alive. It was as good a time as any for Mikey to say the words that came out of his mouth next.

Mikey: "Aww shit man!"

I spun round to clock Sunny, Rab, and the rest of their mob in mighty numbers behind us. Sunny pointed towards the fire exits which were being held open by bouncers, letting cold air into the warehouse. Those were Scott's contacts at the door. Sunny nodded his head to tell us to proceed. I took one look at Snez and Mikey and we collectively sighed as we walked outside into the freezing winter night.

Snez, Mikey and I were rounded up like sheep. Scott and his blood-thirsty goons on one side, with Sunny, Rab, and their mob coming at us from the rear. We stood in the middle of the bumpy, snow-covered tarmac in the carpark, the brick wall of the warehouse behind us, and long stretches of grass ahead of us with hundreds of cars parked up by revellers. The ground beneath us was a slushy, muddy mush.

The 'Angel' track wasn't at its peak yet.

Despite the fire exits being snapped shut, it was loud enough to feel like this insane situation was happening in a club.

The three of us stood back-to-back between the blood thirsty goons and the violent mob. Sunny and Scott locked eyes for the first time. Rab stood at Sunny's side holding his serrated machete, his caveman glare intent on causing alarm. The operatic chanting from the track continued. Fear pulsated between Snez, Mikey, and I as we stood in the middle of it all just waiting for things to take a sinister turn. I could feel the heavy breathing of my boys as their backs grazed against mine. It got claustrophobic as both sides moved in closer, stopped only by Scott having the first say.

Scott: "Well then. You lot look like the boys who broke up my wee rave at Ingliston!"

Scott had come ready to fight, wearing a *Superman* t-shirt to show off his hulking physique. His goons were an assortment of bald bruisers and steroid monsters. Their foes standing behind Sunny and Rab were in a menacing uniform of all black including their balaclavas. Snez, Mikey, and I had a gut-wrenching *deja vu* from the night we got ambushed. Sunny had upgraded his walking cane and pointed it at Scott.

Sunny: "And you look like the dobber who's gonnae pay me a lot of cash!"

Rab kept glaring.

There was no way out.

Scott casually placed his hands on his hips and let out a pretentious laugh: "Ha! You sure about that pal? Coz you look like nothing more than one of those wee fannies who parks up at Asda and shows wee lassies what's under his car bonnet."

Rab spat venom and thrust his head forward only stopped by Sunny throwing up his cane. Mikey gave my arm a squeeze as we darted our heads back and forward between Scott's crew and Sunny's.

Sunny: "I think you're jumping the gun here, Scott, isn't it? See we've been hearing a lot about you. Phil's DJ pal, right? I mean that's all you were to us. Superstar DJ. King of Howden. But now look at you. Hitting the big time, eh. Gangster boy! Only, you seem to be missing something of value –"

Scott: "Fucking forget about it mate. If you think these *wasters* have anything over me then you're still just a pound-a-drink, Apple Sourz kinda bawjaws who has no business standing here with the big boys. Away back to Asda in your Honda mate."

Scott's goons erupted with laughter as he stood with an athlete's confidence, hands still firmly on his hips.

Sunny threw his free hand high up into the air, and I swear to God for a moment, we all felt it. The chanting in the track hit its peak as we stared at a disc with a pattern of red love hearts against a milky white background. Scott's disc!

Mikey: "Motherfucker found it!"

For the first time in my life I seen that smug look on Scott's face drain like someone just pulled the plug to his blood supply. His confidence crushed. Sunny kept his arm held high with a smile that stretched right up each side of his face. Even Rab was smiling. But before the violent haggling could commence a smokeball of a car came plunging towards us.

The wasted wizard returned as Catface pulled up, spinning his car to a halt. Doors opened and like a *Stars in Their Eyes* moment Lucas appeared with bat in hand, followed by a very nonchalant Catface who had one fat J in his mouth and one resting on each ear.

Sunny, Rab and their mob at one side.

Snez, Mikey and me in the middle.

Scott and his goons at the other side.

Walking towards us all with his bat held out in front of him was Lucas, with a very baked Catface in tow, who clearly didn't process how fucking serious things were. Lucas stopped just as he reached the crowd. Catface halted just behind him. It was like we were all savage pieces of a vicious chessboard now. Whoever moved first would set off a chain-reaction. Lucas gave a throaty roar.

Sunny, clearly still resentful for the leg smashing at the garage, shouted out.

Sunny: "Catface you cunt!"

Scott: "Catface?"

With a bewildered look Scott shrugged: "Why do they call you Catface?"

But before Catface could answer Lucas screamed: "Nathan, Mikey, it's a fucking set up!"

Snow kept falling.

Mikey: "We know man, *look*."

He pointed at Sunny holding the disc.

Mikey and I shook our heads in confusion and I felt a sickening palpitation. It was all happening so fast.

144

Scott: "Who gives a *fuck* what's happening in your little drama. That's my fucking disc! Good to see you back on your feet, Lucas."

Lucas raged back at him: "I'll fuckin get to you *and* those cunts!"

He pointed his bat right for the goons.

With everyone fraught with emotions we pinned our eyes on Sunny. Scott kept his eyes on his disc, firmly in Sunny's grasp. Mikey held me up from shock, and Catface toked gently behind a bat-wielding Lucas watching it all unfold. Snez stumbled on the frozen tarmac then fell to his knees in front of Mikey and me, as if he was having some kind of PTSD shit.

Sunny faced Scott: "Now it's time to make a deal for *this.*"

He arrogantly held the disc in the air, poised for his final manoeuvre.

You never know what the final spark will be to set off an explosion. As everyone was immersed in the commotion Catface stepped forward and flicked his joint directly into Sunny's eyes which gave off a sizzle and sting leading to the pile on! Scott's goons charged. Sunny's mob charged back at them. Me and Mikey, in the middle of the stampede, threw ourselves to the floor to cover a blubbering Snez who would surely get trampled to death.

[Tunes still blare from inside the club, with the track now in its own final frontier]

[Followed by the track's angelic, operatic chanting]

Mayhem and absolute fucking bedlam ensued! Bodies everywhere. Sunny backed off in a retreat to keep the disc safe as Scott battled through the crowd trying to get to it. I covered Snez as best I could as I pleaded with him to get up. But he couldn't. His spirit was broken. Amongst the clamour came Lucas soaring in with his eyes to the ground, looking for boots that he recognised from his beating in the warehouse. As Sunny's mob and Scott's goons tore strips out of each other like rival wolfpacks, Lucas swung at every goon wearing boots that looked familiar.

Boots flew into my face as I tried to protect Snez. This set Mikey off into a rage before he sprang up, throwing helicopter hooks at anyone who came near. Still I kept pleading with Snez to get up. Practically begging him. Scott worked his way through bodies, using *Kari waza* throws and *Age-Tsuki* punches to deal with opponents until he found himself face to face with Rab and his machete.

Rab lunged at Scott slicing into his arms with the blade. Scott gave him a brutal punch to the throat. It was too fast to keep up with. *Now* we were at Mach 10. They ended up locked together before Scott swiftly reversed him over his shoulder straight down onto the icy ground with a solid smack. Rab's head cracked open. Sunny volleyed abuse from the side-lines. Smug as Scott was he hadn't realised that Rab plunged the machete into the meat of his thigh during the scrap. Scott plummeted. Both were grounded.

Snez torqued his body, pulling me up with him as the fury erupted all around us and punched me straight in the gut, dropping his GTI car keys into my hands so no one could see. He looked in my eyes, both of us red raw, then kissed my forehead.

Snez: "I tax that car gadgie!"

He smiled at me one last time and then ran off. I took a smash to my jaw from one of Sunny's mob before I could chase after him. I tumbled back to the floor. Hands into the slush. I looked up quick as I could, but Snez was gone.

The mob and the goons had just about worn each other down as the glorious track ended. And another one started up just as Sunny limped towards the grounded Scott, leaning on his cane and holding up the disc. Scott still had the machete sticking out of his bloody leg.

Sunny: "Fifteen grand and you can get this precious disc back! This can all end now. I know you've got the cash. I've seen what you're worth. Call your boys off and let's end this now. You get your disc. I get my cash."

Scott spitefully nodded like a man with no other options. Sunny grinned like a victorious champion.

All the while, barely anyone noticed Lucas creeping up behind Sunny. Scott gritted his teeth as he yanked the machete out and fell backwards, writhing in pain, as Sunny turned round to see Lucas waiting to pounce and had no time to react. Lucas revved up his bat in a circular motion as Sunny's mob started getting to their feet one by one. With an almighty swing Lucas broke two hearts at the same time.

CRACK!! The bat sailed past Sunny's face and smashed the disc into smithereens. Sunny and Scott screamed in an almost joined up fashion in utter disbelief.

147

Sunny & Scott: "Noooooooo!!!"

Sunny's mob came roaring towards Lucas alongside Scott's goons. They were going to tear him from limb to limb. And in that surreal moment we heard the next track playing and you honestly couldn't make this shit up. 'Elements' by Neo Cortex blasted out.

Scott: "That's my fucking car!"

ROOOOOAAAARRRRRRR!

A supercar came flying towards the crowd as the track rushed through our souls. The blizzard was as fierce as ever. Time seemed to crawl in slow-motion as Snez drove Scott's Audi TT with no-one knowing where he was heading. The car ploughed through Scott's goons and Sunny's mob, all divebombing out of the way, then Snez smashed headfirst into Sunny, dragging his body underneath the car which only halted when it slammed against the warehouse wall.

Astonishment poisoned everyone. Sunny's dead, mangled body lay underneath the car. Snez was bleeding badly from his head. Thick smoke rolled out from the back of the car. Petrol leaked and a chemical smell hung in the air.

Snez's head weighed him down. With his final gust of strength, he asked a question in a beaten-up voice.

Snez: "Mind that *Street Fighter* competition we had last year gadgies? I was Guile."

Lucas staggered towards Snez.

Lucas: "Aye mate. Of course we remember bro. You beat me in the final."

Lucas grinned at Snez. Our adopted brother.

Snez: "Ha, that's right gadgie. Beat you with a Sonic B –"

BOOM!!! BOOM!!!

The Audi TT exploded into a ferocious fireball. Shards of glass, rubber, and metal catapulted in every direction. Petrol rained down on us as the explosion made ash out of Sunny's body. All around was chaos. The heat from the blast burned our eyes, and I couldn't even hear myself screaming for the shrill ringing in my ears.

With Lucas dragging me and Mikey away from the pandemonium and confusion, I saw something that made me question my sanity. Or someone. Someone watching it all play out. Someone wearing yellow-tinted shades. Stood next to him was Catface.

CHAPTER 10
EIGHT DJ

Chapter Ten: Eight DJ

Smack bang in the middle of the pub sat me, Lucas, and Mikey.

Apart from Mikey's silver tie—fuck knows where he got that—the three of us wore baggy white shirts that didn't fit, black ties and rumpled trousers we only wore to funerals and the rare uninspiring job interview for some shitey call centre job. That same sense of pitiful hopelessness accompanied the trousers no matter which occasion.

The circular wooden table had 'Jake Wiz ere 1996' chiselled into the middle and 'So was Shaz 2002'. The faded beer mats were frayed at the corners. Smoke lingered in the air, broken up by solitary beams of light. There was a drunk man at the bar putting the world to rights, and an ancient man with a border collie sitting at the far table. The landlady filled up a bowl of water for his dog. A stressed-out looking man sat scribbling away on some paper working out his bets.

An unused vintage brick fireplace faced the bar. Grayscale pictures of the 'good old days' were dotted around the walls. A small, pudgy guy at the end of the bar with grey hair and glasses peeked up at the TV in the corner. Then he hopped off the bar stool, which was much too high for him, to close the window that we just opened.

Snez's wake. His whole life coming down to this moment. A handful of people at the service followed by just us three at the after party. We're the only ones close to counting as family there for him. It was a drizzly, colourless Friday in December. The kind you forget in a hurry. A nothing kind of day. Safer in the pub than it is outside. Most of the snow had melted away. Sunny's funeral was the day before. We didn't go. The hearsay spreading around town is that his mob boosted right after Rezerection. Only Rab turned up at the funeral with the rest of Sunny's family. That's what we heard anyway.

Lucas: "Snez went out like a champion, lads. Like a true warrior!"

We all clinked our drinks together to say cheers to that. It felt fucking pitiful that he had hardly any family to send him off. He deserved better. His whole life he deserved better.

No idea how Scott was. The only reason we hadn't had any shit from him n' his crew yet was due to the fact his car was caught up in the deaths of Sunny and Snez. We all fucked off before the police arrived, but Scott was snookered. Apparently he made sure the club's CCTV was wiped sterile. I was sure it was all going to catch up to us. But I was too melancholy and past caring. We couldn't unsee the things we saw at Rezerection. We couldn't articulate that shit if we tried. All I wanted to do was stare into the puddle of beer at the bottom of my filthy pint glass and just think about Snez.

I swivelled the flat beer round trying to make sense of it all. Lucas was on the vodkas and had already made best pals with everyone in the pub. Eating Noddy's Nuts, Scampi Fries, and rotating between games of pool on a questionable pool table or the pub quiz machine tucked away in the corner of the room. Everything about it felt depressing. Lucas had been nipping at every cunt. I'd hit the giggles at one point and couldn't explain why. Mikey was just sinking into himself.

"What you having love?" said the busty middle-aged barwoman as I staggered back up to the bar. She was cheery and had long curly blonde 80s-look hair. Still she was a nice woman, even though I was so drunk I saw two of her. That's what happens when I cannae afford charlie. Pished drunk after a few pints. Think I preferred the 4am cocaine paranoia if truth be told.

Mikey: "I'll get this one."

He intervened ordering JD and coke. Lucas was outside now jabbering away on the phone. He walked back in with his hair wet from the rain and slapped his hands together.

Lucas: "Sorted boys! Aahahaha."

He went and ticked more charlie fae Gumball. It's the only way we knew how to survive these occasions. Mikey crawled back to the table. I bounced back down with the JD and coke. The three of us sat waiting for Gumball to arrive. Lucas had just hung up the call, but we now stared at his silver Nokia in anticipation for the text that would read 'dive out mate.' There really are only two reasons to stare at a Nokia. One is to watch someone playing *Snake*, the other is to wait for your dealer to tell you he's outside.

Lucas: "Cunt better hurry up, I've only got 30p credit left so I cannae keep texting him."

I downed my JD and coke hoping to tackle the depression, but the effects were pale at best. The dunt I was chasing was drifting out to sea. Time seemed to stretch right out as we waited for the ching. And it didn't stop the inevitable coming up. The questions we danced around since that crazy night.

I lifted my head from my glass and opened the can of worms.

Me: "Why'd you do it Lucas?"

Mikey groaned, looking away from the conversation as if that would protect him.

Lucas paused, and scanned the pub: "Are you for real? I come back to bail you cunts out and you still want to give me grief over the fuckin disc!"

Me: "It was the only leverage we had man!"

Lucas: "It was killing us. Just look at the state of us man. Take a look at that cunt—points at Mikey— look at my napper, look at the state of *you*! That disc did us no good since the moment you got it. It didnae lead us to Phil man. It led us here, to this wake. Snez is dead, Phil is dead, and we're all gonnae be next if we dinnae get the fuck out of here."

Me: "I told you already, Phil was *there* that night. I saw him with Catface!"

By now Mikey was trying in vain to avoid looking at us. Without opiates the lad just cudnae handle this shit.

His fingernails were bitten to the bone, a tell-tale sign he was off the pills.

Lucas: "Nathan for fuck sake, how many times? Phil *wasnae* there! No one else saw him. You were fuckin tripping man. It's understandable, look how much shit was going on. The shock of watching Snez die. The chaos. No wonder you were so confused."

I shook my head with a grimace on my face and gritted my teeth.

Me: "I'm not fuckin confused. We *need* to go and ask Catface where he went that night. Convenient how he disappeared right after it. It's up tae you brother. Make your choice. I'll do it alone if I need to."

Just to get my point across that wee bit better I pounded the table hard with my fist, making an assortment of empty beer glasses clank together.

Lucas's stool scraped against the floor as he stood up ready to pounce.

Mikey: "C'mooon man, c'mooon. Just stop! Both of you. Just stop, please."

The pub grew silent. Lucas snarled.

Lucas: "Fuck the disc. Fuck it all bro!"

Ding ding! Ding ding!

'Dive out mate.'

Gumball was outside. Thank fuck for that. Lucas wasted no time, whilst Mikey made a stealth walk to the bar for another round of pints. I gulped down half of mine.

"Hallo."

I looked up from my beer to see Cassie.

My mouth hung open, but my brain wouldn't compute. Mikey rolled his eyes and kept looking for

Lucas. He hated any form of awkwardness. It made *him* feel awkward.

Cassie: "Well nice to see you too, hey."

She stood before me with telling eyes and powdery blue eye shadow. She wore a brand-new pink leather jacket and a wide sexy smile. Cassie radiated pure goodness and still knocked the wind out of me with just her smile. Which posed the question: What the fuck was she doing here to see me?

Lucas pushed his way through the double door entrance wild-west style back into the pub, hung outside the toilets and with a simple 'hello nod' he acknowledged Cassie. Then he gave Mikey and I the 'cocaine nod.' Mikey darted across the floor like a shot to go and powder his nose with Lucas. Cassie sat down.

Me: "Cass, what you doing here?"

I shook my head in self-pity.

Me: "All I do is cause you shit. I cannae even afford to sort you a new car out."

I could barely look at her for the shame.

Cassie: "Well this is a typical response then, hey? Drown in a stupid pint and push me away. I just came here to tell you I am sorry about your friend. Snaz, was it?"

I burst out laughing.

Me: "Snez. His name was Snez."

Cassie: "Oh right, Snez. Sorry I barely met the guy. But I can see how much he meant to you."

I started getting anxious. Mostly because I knew Lucas and Mikey would be in the toilets like a Dyson hoovering up the charlie. I was desperate for a fat line. So much that it was like mental jumping jacks trying to concentrate on Cassie's words. But she was right in front of me reaching out. I rubbed each thumb across my fingers as if playing a xylophone trying to focus on her words and not on the coke that was calling out to me.

Me: "I loved him. He was my brother. And Phil. Phil's…"

I couldn't get the words out.

Cassie: "Talk to me, Nathan. I'm here. I'm listening. That fucking 'shut' they sniffing in the toilets isn't going to solve your problems. You're trapped in a cycle. You do know that, don't you?"

Here was me thinking she couldn't tell how ching-hungry I was.

My head dropped into my hands thinking of the monstrosities I'd caused her. Cassie was a sceptic when it came to self-pity though. She just wouldn't allow it.

Cassie: "Tell you what, go have your stupid line. On one condition, you tell me *everything* when you get back."

She had herself a deal and I gung-ho'd it to the toilets to play catch up.

It was a typical Livi pub toilet. Scratched out mirror above the grotty sinks with a brownish soap bar that you were scared to use. Slow, thirty-year old hand dryer. Grubby red tiles on the floor. Dried-up piss smudged all over it. Obvious to say it stank of pish in there to the point it overpowered the two hapless urinal cakes. There was a solitary rectangular window so high up you'd need a ladder to reach it and you couldn't see through it, much less escape through it in the event of an emergency.

The lack of natural fresh air really helped to contain the smell of shit and puke. Buzzing irritated my ears. It might have been the long, flickering light fixture above my head, which also acted as a cemetery for the skeletal remains of wasps who found their way in but never back out. Their dead bodies bleached by the light. Serves them right, the venomous little fucks.

There were two cubicles. One containing the not-so-incognito duo of Mikey and Lucas banging lines. The other had a broken toilet roll holder with the plastic translucent front hanging by the hinges. All the toilet roll was balled up in the loo, swamp-brown with diarrhoea piled on top of it and splattered inside the toilet. Still, it felt like home. Many a good cocaine binge took place in bogs like this. And that's all I could think about as I thumped the closed cubicle door.

THUMP! THUMP! THUMP!

Me: "It's me ya cunts open up!"

Dull voices: "Me, who?"

Followed by hysterical childish laughter.

Me: "C'mon tae fuck stop being idiots geez a line man. In fact geez two!"

Dull voices: "What's the password?"

More hysterical childish laughter.

Me: "The password is fuckin open up now!"

THUMP! THUMP! THUMP! THUMP!

To the sound of hilarity the door swung open with a *'Call Jonny on this number for blowjobs'* menny in black marker pen, followed by some poor cunt's mobile number. Mikey and Lucas were both laughing so hard it made Lucas cough up phlegm. I didn't give a shit. Bent straight down to the grimy ivory toilet seat and snorted line after line as if it was medication. Well it was in a way. *Now* I was ready to talk to Cassie.

The three of us burst out of that grubby loo as if we were about to enter a disco in *Boogie Nights*. But it was the same uneventful pub from five minutes before. Not to us though. Now everything felt like sparkles and glitter. We were mafia gangsters from the 70s. Rockstars from the 80s. Movie stars from the 90s. Mikey grew ten-foot-tall and tagged along with Lucas, who was now in full-fledged comedian mode, to play some fuzzy old guys at the pool table whilst I sat back down to chat shit to Cassie, who had ordered herself a gin and tonic, and a pint for me.

Cassie: "Right then, *now* are you gonna tell me everything?"

Me: "First, tell me why you are here. Really."

Cassie looked down at her drink.

Cassie: "I've never had family Nathan, not since I was young. I told you this. And as crazy as all you lot are, hey, you are a family."

I nodded as the coke ripped through me.

Me: "Awrite Cass, awrite. But it doesnae get any prettier from here."

I licked my teeth and felt great. My eyes floated in front of my face and I had a permanent smile. The gear provided me with a fresh drumbeat, so I hoped Cassie was ready to sit back and digest it all.

I spilled my guts in full. I told her all about the night we first met. The shit with Sunny n Rab. The mess between Phil and Scott. My big cuz disappearing. The disc. My relationship with the Peruvian dancing dust. Fuck man I told her about Grandad and everything. It's like I'd been wating for this conversation all my life. Something about her, just made it all tumble out.

Cassie didn't falter once. Her attention was steely focused. I told her everything. Right up to the point of seeing Phil with Catface after Snez died. At least I *thought* it was Phil. I was so fucking sure of it. But Lucas gave me doubts.

Me: "What if I was wrong?"

Cassie: "Right, well there's only one way to find out. Drink up. And let's go and see Whiskers."

She did it again. Had me in fits of laughter.

Me: "It's Catface. And you've just had a drink, you cannae drive."

Cassie: "I know it's Catface. You boys aren't the only ones who can crack a joke ya know. And you ain't the only ones who break the rules either."

She knocked her drink back and stood up, willing me to do the same. I looked over at Lucas and Mikey. They were getting tanned by the two fuzzy old guys at pool.

Cassie: "Look, it's now or never. Let's go talk to Catface."

I was starting to think Cassie was getting a second-hand dunt out of all our shenanigans by now.

I wasn't interested in finding out the disastrous effects of bringing Lucas on this goose chase, so I left sharp without telling them. I followed Cassie outside. The drizzly rain had been replaced with plump flakes of snow, quickly adding inches to the ground. We almost jogged before the lads could notice our absence. Cassie's car took me by surprise.

It was a baby-pink Mini. I squeezed into the passenger side onto a slippery leather chair as she slunk into the driver's seat.

Me: "You really like these pink Minis, eh?"

She smiled and winked, then we drove off towards Heatherbank to pay Catface an unexpected visit.

By the time we reached the street of my youth, snow was tumbling down, turning it into a beautiful hazard. God I loved this street so much. It was a literal time capsule, and the snow brightened up the nostalgic feel as it smothered lampposts, bushes, and wheelie bins.

Cassie slowed the car to a halt: "Ready?"

I answered with a plain nod and pulled the door handle to let myself out into the wild.

Cassie: "Stop! Hold on, isn't that the guy over there?"

I snapped my head round, squinting my eyes to see through the falling fluff.

Me: "Good spot!"

Cassie jerked her shoulders up and laughed. I pulled a confused face to ponder how she even knew who he was.

Cassie: "Tattooed guy, right? Looks cool. Stewed?"

Me: "Stewed?"

Cassie: "Well stoned, whatever."

Me: "But how d'you –"

Cassie: "Because girls actually listen, Nathan!"

She was frighteningly accurate. Catface was so baked he was out in the cold wearing nothing but a flimsy yellow V-neck t-shirt showing off his inked-up arms, with bracelets made from beads and blackish-brown rope, and a matching necklace dangling down. Joint in mouth, and one resting on each ear, held in place by a bobbly, grey bunnet. And of course his cherry Doc Martens.

What puzzled us was the beat-up canvas duffle bag he was carrying, which looked too light and flimsy to contain anything. I ducked down and slowly pulled the passenger door shut. Catface wiped fresh snow from the front of his windscreen on a small banger of a car. The same smokeball from Rezerection. My suspicions grew stronger when I noticed how fake the license plate looked. I could swear black masking tape had altered the letters and numbers. Catface lit his fat J, threw the empty duffel bag into the passenger side, jumped into the driver's seat, and pulled away.

My industrial cocaine dunt was starting to dull down. I'd rushed out of the pub so quickly I'd left my treasure behind. I already worried that Mikey and Lucas would hammer it all before I got back. Resented the cunts just at the thought of it. No worse betrayal known to man than your pals taking yer lines. Then I worried they'd notice I was missing and put two and two together. I needed to sharpen up my buzz before it went AWOL on me, and my mood stiffened. Paranoia was always waiting in the same line as your dunt, snarling and eager for a turn.

Me: "Cass, stick a CD on. Something trancey."

Cassie duly obliged and the soundtrack for the stakeout rung from the speakers. Something about this song always took me back to my high school days. Tainted childhood memories of me, Mikey and Snez always fighting the odds. Reminded me of Lucas bailing us out. Reminded me of Phil. Reminded me of that very first time we all partied together. How we thought it would never end. We truly believed we were forever young. The track was '7 Colours (Angelic Remix)' by Lost Witness. A dam burst in my soul, freeing a flood of nostalgia which flowed into a river of dopamine in my brain, merging into one large tsunami that tingled down my entire body as we discreetly followed Catface.

We stayed two car spaces behind as we followed Catface through a flurry of snow coming down fast. Straight ahead. Left turn. Right turn. Straight on. Straight over the roundabout. Right turn. The route was strangely familiar. But it couldn't be… could it?

Me: "If he takes a left turn here am gonnae… what the fuck! What's he doing here?"

Left turn. Straight down a hill. Right turn.

Cassie: "Where now?"

Me: "Just park up here behind these vans. We cannae follow him any further."

Cassie stopped behind a large work van. An alleyway nearby disguised us slightly. We watched on as Catface parked up outside of a building further down the hill. My confusion grew.

It was a large, industrial, white-stoned building with a yellow banner at the top. In bold black writing were the words **'Sunny side up.'**

Me: "Sunny's garage?"

I was absolutely bewildered. Stumped. The garage was empty. Place was white hot after Sunny's death.

Cassie: "What will we do now?"

Me: "Let's just watch and see what happens."

The two of us had our faces practically pressed up against the windscreen on the passenger side peering out. I tightened my face trying to focus my eyes. Between the distance, the van in front of us and the snow it was hard to make sense of what was going on. Catface walked slowly from his motor, lit another joint and carried the empty duffel bag low down next to his left knee. He got to the front of the garage, took one look to his right, then his left, then walked forward.

Me: "Fuck, he must be inside!"

We stepped out of the car.

Cassie and I locked arms as we made our way down the slippery hill. Standing outside the garage gave me goosebumps. I thought back to the day Lucas smashed up Sunny's legs. Then Rab chasing us back up that very hill in his van with their mob. Catface saved us that day. He also helped us at Rezerection.

As I stood there staring at the yellow banner with Sunny's name, in what now felt like a ghostly recall, Catface strolled out and came to a halt right in front of me. The beat-up canvas duffel bag looked heavier than before. Smoke snaked out from his joint and his little beanbag eyes smiled as he slowly lifted his head up.

Catface nodded: "Brethren. Cassie."

Cassie: "Huh? How'd you know my name?"

She took a beamer.

Catface winked: "I pay attention."

I shook my head. I almost didn't want to ask him the question that came out of my mouth. The answer might be too permanent to come back from. My heart was crashing into my chest. I *had* to ask.

Me: "Catface, I love you man. Always have. But I need to let you know that this next question needs an honest answer. All the years I've known you. Everything comes down to this one question. We won't survive this moment if you don't look me in the eye and tell me the truth. Where the fuck is Phil?"

My cheeks were pinched from the cold and my hands red raw. Warm breath left me in gulps and rose into the freezing air like puffy cotton.

Catface: "I'd never hurt you brethren. It hurts my heart that you'd ever think that. We're the same blend of soup. But after what they made Snez do, I understand it compadre. Nothing is as it seems. I'm sorry to be so bizarrely mystic about this. But I'm asking you to trust me."

Me: "I do trust you, brother. Always have. That's why Lucas isnae here with his bat."

Catface nodded: "And a nifty bat it is too."

Cassie: "What is wrong with you silly boys, hey? Always with the bloody violence."

Catface: "Worry not my new friend, I am but a pacifist. And things are about to become a lot clearer."

Catface turned back to me: "You've actually saved me some traversing. I need to give you something. If you truly want to find Phil, you can't open these until you are with your brother and Mikey."

He opened the duffel bag. It knocked the fuckin wind out of me seeing so much cash! Stacks of which neither of us had ever known. I was on complete tenterhooks waiting for Catface to explain himself. He pulled out four envelopes. All of them plain white. He handed me three.

167

Each one had a name on it. Nathan. Mikey. Lucas. It wasn't our names that sent shockwaves through me. It was what was written underneath them: Eight DJ. I gripped them in a pile in my hands and shot a puzzled look at Catface.

Me: "H... h... how's this possible? How... how... wh... –"

Catface: "Nathan, my brother, we've had each other's backs over the years. Never betrayed each other. Trust me one more time. Now I need to go and give this last envelope to Scott."

Catface held up the envelope with Scott's name and the words 'Eight DJ' on it. Just like ours.

He held out his right arm for a hug, whilst still firmly holding the bag of money. I leaned in and hugged him back.

Catface whispered in my ear: "We'll always be two lads fae the scheme, brother. Two lads fae the scheme wae one big dream."

Then he waltzed away in a cloud of smoke.

Cassie looked at me and shrugged as if to ask, 'What now?'

I stood there and watched him drive away. We grew up together in Heatherbank. There wasn't a flippant bone in his body. He was a rare breed. He wasn't exactly part of our drug-drenched group. But the loyalty we had for each other always extended out to Catface and was reciprocated.

I needed to get back to the pub and open these envelopes with my boys.

Cassie didn't mess around. We got back in the mini and stuck the track on repeat as we raced to the pub.

Lucas was already in a rage as we pulled up. He'd been out the front of the pub with Mikey searching for us. Poor bastard was in a state. The nearest lamppost was on the receiving end. He marched up to the car.

Mikey caught up to us: "What's going on man? Where did youz go?"

Lucas grabbed me for a hug but it felt more like a punishment as he near enough cracked my back.

Cassie: "It's about your cousin."

Lucas sprung back from our embrace: "What about him?"

Me: "These."

I held up the envelopes.

There was a double-double-take from Lucas and Mikey.

Cassie: "Guys, what the hell is going on?"

Lucas snatched his envelope mouthing to himself: "Eight DJ?"

Mikey snatched his envelope too. All the while the snow was relentlessness.

Mikey spoke like a man stumbling on salvation: "How is this possible? This must mean that Phil... Phil's *alive*?"

Cassie: "Will someone bloody tell me what Eight DJ means?!"

Chapter Eleven: Fly Away

Lucas sat with his arse on the cold concrete, legs crossed, fag drooping from his lips. His shirt collar flapped around in the wind. Rain washed away the snow and wind dried up the rain. Now it was blowing around our comedowns. Typical fuckin Scottish weather, even in December. Windchimes rattled. Surrounded by the departed souls in Adambrae Cemetery, it was a bizarre setting for an 8am comedown. We never could understand why life dealt us so many losses.

Lucas kept his eyes on the plaque in front of him, a sort of notice board of family members we once had with us. A track chanted out from the Green GTI. Snez's GTI. It was 'On the Beach' by York. Mikey was practically perpendicular in the passenger seat, eyes closed and a smile on his face. Lucas looked over at him and gave a head tilt. Mikey returned with a nod.

Cassie: "You guys don't make any sense to me."

Cassie and I were resting on a memorial bench under a soft blanket.

Me: "How?"

Cassie: "Well, just how you can be so brutal one minute, but so gentle the next."

It never felt like a choice we made. It was always survival. Every day. All we ever wanted was to party and have fun. So I didn't say anything back. I kind of laughed and nodded. After everything Cassie had seen, I didn't exactly have any defence for our actions. It was a tumultuous lifestyle that left us hyper alert and hyper vigilant. But we were never purposely dodgy to anyone. In our version of events, we were always the good guys.

Me: "Isn't it strange?"

Cassie: "What?"

Me: "That it feels more peaceful in this cemetery than it does out there?"

She nodded.

Me: "This life will be over in the blink of an eye."

I'd gone in a bit heavy. But I carried on.

Me: "I mean just look what happened wae Snez. Even Sunny. One day this will all be over. And the question for a lot of people will be: 'What was the fucking point of it all?'"

Cassie: "Jeez you are starting to sound like Mikey, hey. And what will your answer be?"

Me: "Honestly? It used to be trance. But it's not the same anymore. I've got this feeling in my stomach. It's like… like the moment's over. I mean as long as the music exists, trance will never die. But people, they're changing. If you ask me, they've stopped being interesting. Know what I mean? Phil was right. It's happening already. No one lives for the moment anymore. But *we* did. *We* definitely did. And no one can ever take that from us."

Cassie grinned. I think she finally understood. The track ended. The windchimes took their place. Lucas was finishing another fag. Mikey was digging around the glove box. I was running out of time to ask Cassie the question that was nipping at my heid all night. Aye ano it was eight in the morning but if you hadn't been to sleep yet it was still night.

Me: "Cassie, I just need to know, why are you still here with me? All I've done is cause you shit."

Cassie: "Well I dunno if you've ever noticed Nathan, but there ain't exactly a lot of choice for a girl in Livingston, now is there?"

That set us both off laughing.

Me: "Aye well, this is true."

Cassie: "You're lost, Nathan. I'm lost too."

No one had ever said anything like that to me before. It really shook me. I'd never thought of my life that way. See the thing about Cassie was, she had this effect on me. Like she hugged that place in my heart that my grandad used tae hug. Made it tick again. It's the kind of thingwae that's a bit hard for a lad like me to explain. Know what I mean? Makes me stumble my words.

I leaned in and kissed her under the blanket. It *did* feel like a good idea at the time. Mid-kiss, an abrupt and loud cry from Mikey made me laugh, almost right into Cassie's mouth! He was yelling from the car.

Mikey: "Digweeeeed! Digweeeeed!"

What followed was the rush we needed to jump-start the mood. A track that took you to the heart of the trance scene. All over the world people found themselves under strobes and flashing lights to the genius creation of John

Digweed. Bedrock – 'Heaven Scent.' A truly evergreen track that managed to pulsate all our broken feelings through the speakers. It was blissful. No one had to utter a word. You just *felt* it all melt away. A fucking epic release. Perfect timing, Mikey.

Cassie sighed: "Here we go again then, hey?"

We piled into the GTI and headed towards my brother's place. It felt weird to have Lucas driving Snez's car.

Before long we were sat round the living room in a cloud of smoke, drinking beer that our tastebuds were rejecting. The comedown shakes starting for all but Cassie. We ramped up the heating to shield us from spiky jitters. Dealers weren't replying to our desperate pleas for more tick. Depression was looming. Lucas was preparing to dish out the last of the lines.

That's when we began telling Cassie about Eight DJ.

Mikey: "It all began in Deans."

Cassie: "Deans?"

Lucas emptied out the final remains of baggy onto the living room table. My face was twitching already.

Mikey: "Aye Deans. Well St. Andrew's Way specifically."

Cassie: "I'm still not following."

Lucas squeezed the charlie together using a debit card and a driver's license in a vice-grip fashion, then separated it into three lines. Trying to pad them out as much as possible, to trick our brains into thinking the stingy lines were huge. It felt bittersweet. Phil often referred to cocaine as a moreish drug. It was never enough.

Me: "For a wee while the four of us lived in St Andrew's Way. Snez would come and stay over as well. Ha, that was when Snez used to bleach his hair Gazza style to hide the ginger. It was the first time Phil ever thought about trying to go it alone as a DJ."

Cassie: "Right? And?"

Lucas finished. But it was what he was chopping up next to the coke that was distracting me.

Mikey: "That was the first time Phil and Scott fell out. And I dinnae mean a wee tiff. It was a proper break up. Phil was gonnae go it alone. But to be honest with ye Cass, he just never had the confidence to go for it. We encouraged him. I told him if he had his own DJ name it would feel real. I've read up on positive visualisation you know."

Cassie: "OK, OK, so then what happened?"

I was so engrossed with Lucas I'd drifted out of the conversation. Is he *really* doing what I think he's doing?

Mikey: "Eh Nathan? Nathan… Nathan!"

Me: "Eh? What, sorry. What ye askin?"

Cassie: "He is saying that you came up with the name?"

I didn't hear her. Lucas *was* doing what I suspected.

Me: "Bro what the fuck are you doing?!"

Lucas: "I'm not wanting a bangin fuckin headache man. We need to get a good sleep after this. Need to get ready to finally get this prick cousin of ours tonight. And I tell ye something, the cunt better be alive, so I can kick his fuckin baws for everything we've been through."

Lucas was chopping up paracetamol and putting it in the lines of charlie.

177

Cassie: "Nathan would you bloody finish the story, hey!"

Me: "Aye, aye... sorry! Eight DJ. EH54 8DJ. It was the postcode for St Andrew's Way. It was a wee party house we lived in for a few months. Whilst we were there, I told Phil he should call himself Eight DJ. It kindae stood out. Only our own wee inner circle knew the meaning behind it. He loved the idea. That was going to be the big plan. The end game. All of us riding the waves with Eight DJ. No other cunt knew that story. Catface didn't know it. Only us. And Snez... and Scott. Phil got a wee bit cocky one night and chucked the idea in Scott's face."

Cassie: "So why didn't you just tell me this last night when I asked you?"

Mikey: "Cassie, it's like I told Nathan about the discs. Eight DJ, it was Castles in the Sky."

That left Cassie with more questions than answers.

Me, Mikey, and Lucas snorted up our pathetic paracetamol laced lines.

Cassie: "And all the envelopes say that exact same thing inside?"

I placed all three envelopes down on the table.

Each envelope had lyrics scribbled on the inside and a message.

11pm Saturday night lads, we're on the up!

Mikey: "Well fuck knows about Scott's. But aye ours are identical. It's a Chilli Peppers song, Cassie. *Under the Bridge*."

Me: "I've no idea what his plan is. But I know my cousin. No one else would have written this. This has to be him. And there's only one bridge that ever mattered to him. For all the wrong reasons though."

I paused.

Me: "He's going to be at that bridge tonight. Fuckin trouble is though, so will Scott and all his goons."

Lucas picked his envelope up.

Lucas: "That's why I dinnae understand why mine has this on it!"

Written on my brother's envelope was:

Leave the bat at home cuz x

Lucas: "Fuck this shit, youz want to play a game of cuts?"

Mikey and I curled up into protective balls.

Cassie queried what 'cuts' was exactly.

When I told her that cuts was a game of us all cutting ourselves with razor-sharp knives until we each tapped out leaving only one winner—always unanimously Lucas—her reaction was as expected. Equal measures of shock and disgust.

Lucas shrugged.

Lucas: "What?"

For us, cuts was an end of the sesh, a final attempt at a buzz, a mindless game. Got to keep that adrenaline pumping to keep the treacherous hours of comedown away. Thankfully Cassie was with us, otherwise we'd have been playing.

So that was it. The 'night' over. We couldn't stave off the comedown any longer. The options at this stage of a sesh varied depending on your surroundings:

Drug-fuelled, cum-stained shags to appease the coke horn (only under the rare circumstance that you could make your coke dick / eccy-dick get hard again right enough).

Going on the hunt for more gear.

Anxiously waiting for the wastelands of your insides to spew up with bile.

Finding a mirror and speaking directly to your paranoia.

Or try sleeping it off knowing full well you'd be rolling around your bed for hours to come, eventually released from the grip of the uppers then passing out into a haven of lucid dreams and hallucinations that left your bedsheets soaked in sweat. Every now and then waking and trying to brave your way to the toilet to empty your bladder through a hard-on. Pissing so much you may as well be a camel. Too many eccies and you'd feel the piss desperate to evacuate your bladder, but nothing would come out. You'd really have to tap into your inner Jedi to get the piss out. If things were really dire you'd piss into any empty bottles lying in your room, rather than facing the fear of the long walk to the bathroom.

Seeing as we had to meet our cousin at the designated spot later that night, we opted for the forced-sleep marathon. Luckily for Cassie she'd only had drinks so she would pass out quickly. Mikey took the couch. Lucas in his own room. Cassie and I took the spare room.

It was a snare and drum sound on repeat that woke me. The room smelled of days-old curry and nail polish. One eye stretched open. Cassie groaned and woke up too. The sound became more brilliant and familiar. It was vibrating, *no*, it was rumbling up the walls. It gave me all the thrills of being at the shows with my pals pished, or more likely down at the Livi Nitespot on a Thursday night, one pound a drink, eccied out yer face after scoring gear from the bouncers.

'Bits & Pieces' by Artemesia.

Cassie wrapped a pillow around her head and screamed: "Bloody hell! What time is it?!"

I checked my Nokia. 5.23pm. The door kicked open. It was Mikey and Lucas.

Lucas: "Right fucksticks, time to get up!"

Me: "What the fuck man?"

Mikey: "If this is gonnae be our last night together, then we are going out in fuckin style."

Me: "But we're all out of fuckin gear man. This time next week the house will belong to the Bank of Scotland. The fuck we meant to do?"

Lucas: "Lucky I've always had this emergency bottle, wee bro."

He showed me a full bottle of Grant's vodka. Well it was called Glen's now but to us it was still Grant's. A litre bottle. He held it up like an Oscar award.

Mikey: "C'mon man, you know it makes sense."

I was soon gulping cola poisoned by vodka. Cassie sipped on water. She said *someone* needed to keep a straight head. Voddy without the charlie was never a good thing. Say what you want about coke but at least it straightened me up. I was getting pished far too fast. So were Lucas and Mikey. Truth be told there was no optimism about it. Know what I mean?

Mikey drunk-stumbled up to my brother's PC to stick a CD on: 'Fly Away' by Vincent de Moor.

In that moment I understood everything Phil was trying to achieve for us. Why he kept on dreaming, no matter how unlikely the fantasies were. Because when the dreaming stopped, it was the same as a rave being over. Nothing but a comedown and suicidal thoughts. But when the music played, the drugs peaked, and my boys were next to me, nothing else mattered.

Cassie: "Hey you, are you alright?"

She nudged me.

Cassie: "Yes, no, maybe so?"

I loved how many wee sayings she had like that.

Me: "Aye Cassie. I'm OK."

Mikey and Lucas were hugging with emphasis on the back pats to keep it as manly as possible.

It was 10:30pm.

I really couldn't wait any longer. I needed my cousin back. I couldn't believe he would be there. We all needed a miracle.

Cassie kept a protective arm hooked in mine.

Lucas let go of Mikey and picked up his bat.

The moment had a ceremonial vibe to it. He held the bat in front of his face, kept a glare locked on, and then placed it in the corner of the living room.

Lucas: "Right fucksticks, are we ready?"

Mikey: "We need tae put this track on in the car. Who's driving?"

Cassie: "Yeh that will be me, hey, the only sober one here."

I'd have encouraged her to stay out of it. To keep herself safe. But sometimes you can just tell by the look on someone's face that their mind is made up.

Lucas: "So we are turning up to this in a fuckin pink Mini?... Awrite let's dae it!"

CRACKKKK!!!!

As we approached the front door, the sky ripped open. Thunder claps and rain forced its way in, bouncing off everything. We made a mad dash for the car.

CRASSSHHH!

Rain came down ferociously and we could barely see the road. No one uttered a word. Mikey still had the CD in his hand. Lucas had the vodka bottle. But we weren't drinking. We weren't listening to tunes. We drove to the bridge in the pouring rain, dead in the night.

It's a dangerous thing to have a warped love affair with suicide and a bridge for the setting. Most lads I knew growing up had a bridge at some point. Some went back to them often. Trapped between two worlds. Don't want to die. Don't want to live. Don't know what to do, so you go to a bridge. Looking through the steel railings is almost poetic. Sums up how much of a prisoner you feel in life.

In society. Inside your own head. Staring down at nothing but an unforgiving reality.

I've been to many of them. Hoping for a miracle. Praying for an answer. Seeing if God will show up. Seeing if anyone will show up. Wondering if a driver will see you, pull over and offer some life-affirming wisdom. Wave a wand and change your reality for you. But it can be a lonely fucking place. Especially when you get there and there are no answers.

Only two options.

Your mind toys with you: 'Do it! …Don't do it!'

You feel like you've got no way out, but you know every bridge has an exit and you can terminate these feelings instantly. It's like your brain is infested and your heart exhausted. You find a bridge when all hope is gone. When you've run out of options.

The bridge was long, stretching right up the dual carriageway until the rusty railings veered off into thick woods garnished with greenery. Underneath the railings was a drop so steep it made me dizzy to think about. Under that drop was a raging river. Most of the year it was deep and fast-moving but with the weather on this night it was thrashing and sweeping away everything in its path. This was a bad omen man. Or as Catface would have said, some bad fucking Juju.

We shouted to hear each other over the relentless rain and the river below.

Cassie: "Where do I stop guys? Can anyone see anything?"

We desperately tried to catch a glimpse of something. Anything. But it was impossible. Lightning flashed to the point we were temporarily glowing inside the car. And then... it couldn't be. Could it?

Me: "Holy fuck. Is that, is that Phil?"

Lucas: "Where?!"

Mikey: "I cannae see a thing man, where is he?!"

We flew from the car and Cassie followed, creeping behind us with her headlights providing just enough light. Rain hammered us. Each footstep sunk into deep puddles. We could hear the sound of tree limbs snapping below. My heart stopped. And I swear to God, we all felt it.

Me: "Phillllll!!!"

Cassie hit the brakes. The headlights revealed a silhouette on the bridge railings. It looked like Phil. Our hope became contagious. All the while our senses were thrown completely off balance by competing sounds of the river, thunder, and the rain, with flashes of lightning intermittently blinding us.

With Lucas and Mikey next to me, I raised my hand over my eyes to improve my vision.

Me: "Phil?"

"Aahaha *really?* You *really* thought that prick was going to be here?"

It was Scott. That bastard. I felt sick to my stomach.

He hopped down from the railings, his leg still stiff from the machete blow. The rain bounced off his brown leather coat.

CRACCCKKKK!!!

Lucas: "I fuckin knew it!"

Lucas flew for Scott but Mikey and I pulled him back.

Me: "Think bro, think!

Scott: "Well would you look at this. I turn up here in good fucking faith, without the cavalry and it's clearly a set up!"

Lucas: "Aye a set up by you ya cunt!"

Scott held up an envelope, just like ours.

Scott: "Eight DJ. I always thought it was a stupid name. So I take it you lot got one of these as well then, eh? Well I had to fucking see it for myself."

We looked around. True to his word, Scott had come alone.

Lucas: "So what then, you actually want to sort this shit out once and for all then? I've no forgotten the warehouse!"

Scott: "Aye and I've no forgotten the fuck ups!"

Mikey: "Where does this all end man? For fuck sake, just tell us what happened to Phil?"

The rain started to let up.

Scott replied with that half smile of his.

Scott: "You know what's always been so fucking hilarious to me? You lot see yourself as the good guys. What's Phil then? The hero? The martyr? You any idea how many times he screwed things up for me? Well? Do you?!"

Mikey shook his head: "It was never supposed to be this way."

Scott: "It's too late for all that. First you lot stole my discs. Then youz leave me with a shit show of affairs hanging over my head. Polis are all over me for what happened with Snez and Sunny. So I'm the monster, eh. Have you boys forgotten what Phil meant to me?"

Mikey: "So feeding me pills through Erica, that made you a good cunt then?"

Scott: "C'mon mate. You hardly fought her off, did you?"

Lucas: "Aye and what about those cowardly cunts who tried to kill me in the warehouse?!"

Scott: "What choice did I have? I needed the discs. I'm in deep lads."

Lucas: "How about fuck those guys. How about that?!"

Scott: "You don't want to mess with these kind of people Lucas!"

Me: "So then you shudda trusted Phil! The two of youz, youz were so close to making it!"

Scott: "Phil kept fucking it all up every time we got close to making it. Time was running out. When the money came my way, I took it. And I'm not sorry. I'm not fucking sorry, OK!"

Mikey: "Well it's not too late to do the right thing man!"

Scott laughed and shook his head.

Scott: "Don't be fucking crazy, I've no way out now! You don't *get* an out! And it wasn't just the discs. It was Phil. He *wouldn't* let it go once he found out."

Me: "Found out what?!"

RATT flashed before my eyes. The two of them going at it in the rave.

Scott: "The studio lads. The studio."

Lucas: "The fuck has that got to do with anything?"

Scott: "Everything. We put it in Phil's name. The rest of it was out of my control. I just took my cut and kept my mouth shut. Turned up, made my tracks, kept it ticking over."

Lucas: "You sell out cunt!"

Scott: "Once I was in with them it was too late. There was nothing I could do!"

Mikey: "So you left the paper trail on Phil?"

Scott stood silent. The rain had stopped completely now.

Me: "And the discs, they were just for show too?"

Scott: "Fuck youz! Those discs were the only *real* thing I ever had. But Phil had me over a barrel. He made me bring them to RATT or he was going to out me over the studio."

He couldn't hide the resentment in his voice.

I had an epiphany.

Me: "You know something, the raves were never supposed to be about making it. They were supposed to be about freedom."

SPLOOOOSSSSHHHH!

A van pulled up next to Cassie's Mini. We all turned. The only one who recognised the van was me. It was Gumball's.

He stepped out.

Me: "Gumball? What *you* doing here?!"

The passenger door opened. Oh my God. It was Phil. It was really Phil!

My first reaction was joy, which got mixed up with confusion. Lucas flew for Phil.

Lucas: "Where the fuck have you been cuz? Where?!"

Scott watched on shaking his head in disbelief.

Phil: "I've been away cuz, trying to sort this out. Trying to get us out of this never-ending world of shit."

Lucas: "Have you any fuckin idea what we've been through?!"

Phil: "I had nae idea until I got back cuz, nae idea at all. That's why am doing this. There's only one way man. Only one way."

I jumped in.

Me: "I fuckin love you cuz, but for fuck sake dinnae do that shit again!"

Mikey: "I thought you'd died man. I really thought you'd died."

Scott: "Well I fuckin didnae. Predictable as ever Phil!"

Lucas grabbed Phil by the face.

Lucas: "Where the FUCK have you been man?"

The reunion was precious for time. Scott hadn't joined the beautiful melee but watched on. Phil untangled his body from ours and approached Scott.

Phil: "You mind that first night when we played Room At The Top? There was a power cut. We knew the crowd was about to hit a comedown any minute. We were still newbies man. Everyone was talking about NEOGENIC. The local duo on the rise. It was our big chance. So we had to do something an–"

Scott cut him off, with a laugh. But it wasn't smarmy this time. It was the most sincere, heartfelt laugh I'd heard from Scott in years: "I remember Phil. I had to reboot everything when the power came back on, and you chanted –"

Phil: "Here we, here we, HERE WE FUCKING GO!"

Scott's face was funereal: "Here we fuckin go man. Here we fuckin go."

Phil: "I knew you were still in there man."

Scott spoke with urgency now.

Scott: "Phil, it's too late for all this shit, they're going to kill you!"

Phil turned to face us: "I tried to sort it out at RATT lads. Nathan, you were so fucked with the charlie."

I nodded. Rock in my throat.

Phil: "Mikey, the pills man, they had you by the baws."

Mikey rubbed his tired eyes with his hands, taking it in.

Phil: "Lucas, you mad cunt. You'd try and kill an army to keep us all safe. But it was killing you too cuz."

Lucas gulped and tried to shrug it off.

Phil pulled something out. A black disc intertwined with luminous yellow in a spiral design. His disc was back in the hands of its rightful owner.

Phil: "Catface told me about the studio. You know that cunt knows everyone. I swore him to secrecy. This was my in, my chance at making a punt for it. We were gonnae be on the up boys! I hid out at Gumball's for a while. I knew that cunt was the only one you'd never go asking. Told his gormless bird I'd dob them in if they didn't help me out. Bye bye to yer easy life sweetheart, kindae thing. Then I took a trip lads. A trip somewhere we've *always* dreamed about."

Lucas: "Why didnae you just fuckin tell us cuz. We coulda handled the truth!"

Phil: "Nae offence cuz but I know your way of handling things. Always wae the bat."

Mikey: "I mean it kinda happened anyway Phil."

Phil: "Ano lads, am sorry. I was getting things in order, but by the time I got back everything was a mess. I know youz wudda been looking for me lads and I love you for it. Don't ever forget that. I was just trying to sort shit out for us all."

We all stood there lost for words.

Phil: "I'm sorry bout Snez. I am so sorry lads. I wanted him to come with us. As soon as I got back Gumball told me everything and he told me about the Rez. I knew shit was gonnae go down there. So I came, but I was too late. Watching him die was the last straw. I knew even if we ran we'd never be free of it. In that moment I knew exactly what I had to do. I grabbed Catface and told him to get me out of dodge. But I've got it all figured out now. Just remember, I love ye. I will always love ye. We're on the up!"

Phil hopped over the railings.

Me: "Wooah what the fuck are you doing ya madman?!"

Phil: "He already said it, lads. They're gonnae kill youz."

His body shivered but he had a tragically special smile on his face, like a lad who always knew that one day it would come down to this for someone like him.

Scott: "Phil, no! Why this? Why like this?"

Lucas grabbed onto Phil's arm. Mikey grabbed the other.

Phil asked Scott an honest question.

Phil: "Are you ever gonnae let us go? Are those mad cunts you're with ever gonnae let us be now?"

Scott delayed, before shaking his head no.

It was like an out-of-body experience. Our minds trying to keep up with the pace of events. Equilibrium distorted. Reality blurred. Spacetime fractured.

Scott: "They can't let youz go now lads. There's fuck all I can even do about it now. But just tell me one thing Phil, why the fuck like this?"

Phil looked at Scott with eyes that said: 'It's all over.'

Lucas: "Cuz don't be a fuckin idiot!"

Phil: "I promised youz I'd make the dream come true cuz."

Lucas: "We'll find another way cuz. But not like this. Never like this!"

We all pleaded with him. Well apart from Scott. He shook his head. But it felt like there was at least part of him that wanted to say something more.

Phil: "You really think we can find another way around all this?"

Lucas: "Fuck aye! C'mon man. Don't be fuckin stupid. Just take my hand and let me pull you back over."

Phil sighed.

Phil: "Awrite cuz, awrite. Just let me go lads. Let me climb back over."

We released the grip. We held out our hands. In the chaos of it, Phil's disc plummeted to the water below.

He looked over at Scott.

Phil: "They'll never let us be free, boys."

Phil released his grip of the bars and tumbled backwards. Lucas and I rushed back toward the railings, but it was too late. He fell faster than I could ever have imagined. It was like he was gone in a flash. We screamed down at the water. Even Scott looked shell-shocked.

Lucas: "Phil!!!"

Me: "Oh my fuckin God, he did it."

Lucas started kicking in the railings.

Lucas: "You cunt. You cunt. You stupid cunt Phil!"

Mikey sank to his knees.

Lucas flew for Scott.

Lucas: "This is you ya cunt, you coulda stopped this. You coulda stopped this!"

Before Lucas could land those blows, we were raided by an army of blue flashing lights and officers in black. Lothian and Borders's finest. They came out of nowhere.

We later learned that Phil had set Scott and his goons up. Accomplished with the help of Erica. It was her attempt at making amends with Mikey. She'd called the police to warn of the impending murder of Phil. Told them everything about the studio, Sunny's garage, even Gumball. Dobbed every cunt right in. After Rezerection, they were already keeping a close eye on Scott. We were all too busy playing cardboard gangsters to even realise that we were under surveillance.

So why did he do it? Maybe coz every good trance track has a catchy build-up before it peaks. It pulls you in and yer hooked. Like the DJ knows everything you're feeling inside. They've found a way to speak to yer soul.

But the peak, aww the peak man, it has to be out of this world to be a classic. It has to be over the top. It has to be fantasy. Euphoria. Unforgettable. It takes you to another world. Nostalgia bubble wrapped. A true trance track lives on in mythology for the rest of time. Maybe that's how he wanted to go out.

Fuck knows. I've agonised over that moment too much. Analysed it and dissected it in every which way but I still couldn't get it to add up. I guess Phil knew it was the only way to keep us all alive. By the time everyone was released from police custody, we'd figured out that Scott was remanded. Tied up in the deaths of Sunny, Snez, and now Phil. The laundering at the studio, even Sunny's dodgy schemes from the garage. We'd stuck to our 'no comment' replies. After all Grandad taught us well. 'Deny, deny, deny' he would always remind us when it came to the pigs.

But it was too late for Scott. He was drowning in it all. Some of the goons were arrested then remanded too but then they evaporated into thin air along with the upper echelons who had silently used Scott like a marionette. They moved on to their next town. Their next victim. Leaving Scott to face the music. How ironic. The studio was left in the hands of some legal cunts. Even that poor schmuck Gumball got busted. I felt sorry for him. Not so much his bird.

I won't lie, once we were released the grieving hit us hard. There was no numbing shock period, just a one-way express to pain. We had to wait for the polis to find the body before we could even plan a funeral. The heat was off us, but there was still part of the story missing.

Something Phil forgot to tell us. But we'd soon find out in the only setting appropriate.

At Resident Raverz.

CHAPTER 12
RESIDENTRAVERZ

Chapter Twelve: Resident Raverz!

A paper tower formed at the front door of Lucas's house:
    Reminders
    Mild warning letters
    Strict warning letters
    Severe warning letters
    And then
    'We're coming for the house soon bawbags' letters.

These were strategically ignored and piled up like a dejected game of Jenga. Opening one of the letters would see the rest of them tumbling down, mirroring the situation we were in with the house. A house that once belonged to our grandparents. They had wanted it to remain in our family. But Grandad left a bit of debt. Lucas added to the debt somewhat. We all did. Now we were officially squatters.

But it was the night of Resident Raverz. One last rave to celebrate Phil and Snez before we disappeared for good.

We had a rough idea of where Phil had set things up for us but couldn't be 100% sure. I'd tell you where we were going, but Lucas gave the strict order that we tell no cunt. Sorry about that. We just wanted a fresh start. To be honest, we had no other choice. We'd run out of shitey jobs, shitey flats, Wonga loans, tick bills, dealers, second chances, third chances, money, and drugs. And of course, the house. Thank fuck for Cassie or none of us would have had enough cash for our last hoorah. Our celebration of Phil and Snez at Resident Raverz. Or our travel money to get out of Livi. We had to hope Phil had really set shit up for us because we would be turning up with fuck all to our names. But before all that, we had one more sesh, one more rave.

I think you know the drill by now.

Pre-rave sesh at my brother's gaff, minus the gear which we were still on the cold turkey from. Tunes, vodka, bucky, MD 20/20, beers, shirts, aftershave, and hair gel. Jump in the Mini, tunes blaring, speeding, pull up outside the warehouse. Step out of the car and unite with our tribe. Fellow ravers at Resident Raverz.

I closed my eyes and inhaled the aura of rave and trance. But there was something niggling at me, and I couldn't shake it. Like that feeling you get when you've forgotten your wallet. Only worse. It was more like something chewing and gnawing at my internal organs.

Lucas slapped his hand on my shoulder: "You ready, wee bro?!"

Me: "Aye brother. Let's do this man."

I lifted up my Stella. Lucas lifted his too. Mikey and Cassie followed suit.

Mikey clinked his bottle into the rest: "For Phil and Snez."

The rest of us repeated: "For Phil and Snez!!!"

The place was bouncing, and the tunes creeped out from the warehouse. Every few minutes the line shuffled down a bit and I spotted waltzers behind the chain-link fencing. Looked a right fucking buzz. They were situated just outside of the warehouse, in between other stalls, tents, and elated revellers. I heard the screams from folk off their tits being spun into the sound of fast trance whilst being blasted with neon streaks of blue, red, green, yellow and pink.

I nudged Cassie: "Ye up for it?"

Cassie: "Of course!"

Mikey: "Ha aye right Nathan, you spewed yer ringer last time you went on those."

Me: "Ano man, but this might be the last time we're at a rave in Scotland, so am going for it."

Lucas: "Ha let's dae it then. For Phil and Snez!"

We were drunk and lairy so everything we did was dedicated to Phil and Snez.

I pulled out a Lambert & Butler and slid it between my lips as soon as we passed the bouncer check. I soaked in the sound of everyone around me. Most of them already on bottles of water. It felt like home.

Cassie: "So are we going on these waltzers then?"

Lucas: "Nah man, first we rave, check out the birds, *then* we come back out for the waltzers."

We made our way inside to the sound of 'Greece 2000' by Three Drives On A Vinyl. The sort of track that took you to a place filled with shots, sunshine, and party people. We stepped onto the concrete dancefloor. Lights down low, orange lasers hanging stationary, cutting

201

through the darkness as the four of us huddled in together. Swarms of people around us. The track was building, gradually getting louder and more intense. Pink smoke machines pumped marshmallow clouds into the worshipping crowd, and flames shot up into the air. Then… the… beat… dropped! It was beautifully deafening. Orange lasers set free to dance around. Hands in the airrrrr!!! Strobes! Ecstasy!

The four of us were as carefree as we'd ever been on this journey together. The crowd roared and I swear to God, we all felt it.

We all laughed. And danced. It felt fucking amazing. As we revelled in the moment another classic trance track started up and it made everything flash before my eyes. The track was 'Carte Blanche' by Veracocha.

It was a healing. Therapy. Thank God for these DJs. They saved so many of us.

I stood there looking at the three of them. I knew that this really was our last moment in this lifestyle.

Cassie threw her arms around my neck: "Waltzers?"

Lucas: "Let's go fuckstick. Cannae wait to watch you spill your guts, bro."

We all laughed at the premonition as we made our way back outside. Everyone around us was full of joy. It was alive in atmosphere, rich in character, loud in energy. But I still had that niggly feeling tugging on my insides. I ignored it. We could hear the guy in the middle of the waltzers shouting through the mic:

Somebody screammm!!!!!
Aaaaaahhhhhhh!!!

Here we go, here we go!!
Everybody scream!!!

An absolute invasion of strobe lights, lasers, and heavy beats as the cars on the ride flashed round and round at a sickening speed. People screaming, some in utter joy, others in panic as the queasiness took over. A middle-aged guy wearing a high-viz top, with long curly hair and the name 'Brian' tattooed on his fingers, was weaving in and out of spinning cars, with him spinning them all into oblivion. We joined the que standing underneath a well-lit flashing sign with the name of the ride. THE ANNIHILATOR!

Let's get ready, here we go!!!

The ride stopped. The man on the mic hidden away like the *Wizard of Oz* in the middle of the ride reminding everyone to take caution as they exited.

Remember to wait for the ride to stop please folks. Here we go!

Just as we stepped on to the ride, I could see why Lucas was distracted. He was making eyes with a tidy blonde across at a wee stall selling shots and laughing gas. She waved him over. Me and Cassie were bundled into a car, followed by Mikey, with Cassie sandwiched between us. Lucas stood with one foot on the ride and one foot off. He was giving his best flirty sign-language to the tidy blonde and then looked over at us with a grin.

Me: "C'mon bro, dinnae make me do this on my own! Ha!"

Lucas: "Sorry wee bro, gottae go chat to this lassie. You know how it is man."

As the steel bar was thrust down, locking us in, Lucas jumped off the ride and flirt-walked over to his new pal. Before I could give him pelters and a bit of banter, high-vis Brian spun our car around in preparation for what was to come.

Heerrrrre we go! Everybody scream!!!!
'Aaaaaaaaggghhhhh!'

The ride spun into motion. Each individual car in a super spin. I was catching glimpses of Lucas as he embraced the girl. Cassie roared with laughter and clutched on to me and Mikey. 'Gouryella' by Gouryella belted from the speakers, as we spun round. And round. And round.

Every few seconds our car would spin past the entrance, and I'd catch Lucas chatting to the girl. People screamed in joy and terror. Lasers flashed. It got so fast that we were pinned to the solid plastic behind our backs. As we spun past Lucas for what felt like the eleventh time, I caught a glimpse of the crowd around him. I nearly choked on my own heart. I did all I could think of. I screamed.

Me: "Stoppppp!!! Stop the ride! Stopppp!"

I tried to catch the attention of high-viz Brian, but he screamed back and spun our car faster. I counted the seconds. 1, 2, 3, 4... another glimpse!

Everybody screammm!!!!

I had to get off. Lucas. Fuck. Lucas! Even Cassie and Mikey couldn't make me out. Our heads were bobbing about with such intensity, I couldn't even lift mine long enough to face them. All I could do was catch a glimpse every four seconds and watch.

It was Rab, stalking my brother.

Gouryella was now the soundtrack to the horror show unfolding before me.

Here we go, here we go! I wanna hear you make some noise!!
  'Aaaaaggghhh'
  Louder!!
  'Aaaaagggghhhhh'

1, 2 , 3, 4… glimpse. 1, 2, 3, 4… glimpse. 1, 2, 3, 4… they were gone! 1, 2, 3, 4… the ride started to slow down. 1… 2… 3… 4… 5… 6… 7… 8… 9… the ride stopped. We weren't where we started. The ride came to a stop halfway round, with me wriggling out of the car in desperation, trying to get the words out to Cassie and Mikey. All I could do was say:

Me: "Rab! Rab! Rab!"

High-vis Brian: "Whoooa, hold yer horses, kid. Lemme let you out first."

As soon as that bar lifted, the three of us sprinted down the steel steps onto the soggy grass, bumping into people who were oblivious to our cause. Lucas wasn't at the stall. The tidy blonde was gone. We looked left. We looked right. We couldn't see him anywhere. There was a brief reprieve when we saw two folk winching in a corner, only to realise with terror that it wasn't Lucas and the bird.

Mikey: "Youz go right. I'll go left, hurry!"

I could hear the end of 'Gouryella' playing as Cassie and I ran for it. Mikey went left. All I could think was 'not again, not again, please God no, not again.'

We covered every inch of grass outside of the warehouse looking for him. Checked stalls, portaloos, and rave tents. Nothing. Eventually we jumped back inside, but it was a fucking needle in a haystack man.

Turns out it was Mikey who found him.

Mikey discovered the only alleyway there was and took a punt at it. Thank God he did because Rab was escorting Lucas into darkness, machete poking into his throat, drawing blood. Mikey had to think fast.

Mikey: "Sunny shouldnae have died that night!"

His words bounced off the brick walls and Rab came to a halt. Lucas still captive. Distant beats and flashes of light from the rave shot into the alleyway.

Mikey: "Dinnae do this Rab. If you do this, you will never be free of it. Trust me man."

Rab pinned Lucas to the brick wall with the tip of the blade placed on his jugular vein. The ground below their feet was grey, wet, and uneven. Lucas wasn't saying a word.

The track following them into the alleyway was Paul van Dyk – 'Nothing But You.'

Rab was unable to hide from his face a crazed man at the end of his tether. But more than that, he was distraught. The machete shaking in his hand.

Mikey tested Rab's resolve with slow steps forward. Creeping ever so slightly closer. Lucas could do no more than speak to Mikey with his eyes. Mikey spoke back in the same way. Trying to reassure him.

Rab: "I told ye this wasn't over, Lucas. I told ye!"

Lucas couldn't reply. The serrated machete was sharp enough to remove his Adam's apple if he did.

Rab: "Sunny was my best mate. The only real mate I ever had!"

The music kept playing. No one budged.

Rab: "After everything he went through, to go out like that!"

Mikey was acutely aware of how easily things could take a turn, so he spoke with urgency: "If you kill him, the cycle never ends. Take that knife off his neck man. Otherwise, we're all gonnae end up dead, in jail, or still doing this shit in our fucking fifties."

Rab seemed to ponder his options. Lucas breathed as shallow as he could.

Just then a quiet voice spoke:

"It's true compadre, a shaman told me all about this one night while we drank mushroom tea."

It was Catface, with a joint dangling from his lips, and one resting on each ear. He carried a beaten-up duffle bag, opened, with more money than you could count.

Catface: "In fact amigo, you could say our hard and fast journey out of Rezerection that night is applicable here."

Herein lies the part of the story that Phil forgot to tell us about on the bridge. Catface explained for the benefit of Lucas and Mikey.

After Snez and Sunny died at Rezerection, and Phil turned up too late, a severely injured Rab was desperately trying to crawl away from the scene. But he was barely making any ground. He was vulnerable to revenge from Scott's goons, or from being picked up by the police. Either way he was a dead man. This was Phil's lightning bolt. Phil and Catface, they saved Rab, in exchange for keys to the garage. They knew there was a lot of cash in that garage, and they knew Rab couldn't go near it without exposing himself. But Catface could. No one was ever on his tail.

And here we all found ourselves. Cassie and me searching inside the rave. Rab with a blade to the throat of Lucas. Mikey the negotiator. Catface turning up with the cash.

Rab whispered: "You've nae idea how far Sunny and I came. We had no choice."

Mikey: "Well, you do now."

Catface causally stepped forward, pulled out a plastic carrier bag, and held the duffel bag out: "You know the deal, good sir. Half of this is yours. Half of it is theirs. Take your half. It's over."

Catface toked hard, no-hands style, with little beanbag eyes.

Rab released his clench on the machete, until it slipped from his hand and fell to the concrete with a clang. He stumbled away from Lucas. He was like a man who had been released from the grip of madness. Lucas reacted the only way he could think of. He tilted his head with a 'we're sound now' nod. Rab returned the gesture. No words were exchanged.

Catface slowly counted Rab's cash into the plastic carrier bag then handed it to him.

Rab peered into the bag and carried out a prompt mental head count.

Catface: "All good?"

Rab nodded. Then he turned around and walked away, leaving the machete behind as if nothing had happened.

Lucas ditched the machete in a wheelie bin on the way out. His gratitude for Catface reached new heights, but they didn't stand around to unpack the events. Instead they waltzed back into the rave to find us. As they retold the close encounter, we pledged not to leave each other's side again until we set foot in... ah I still cannae tell you where, sorry.

It was beyond our wildest dreams to see so much cash.

Me, Cassie, Mikey, Lucas and Catface stood hugging under the strobe lights and flashing lasers. Lucas must have repeated a hundred times how he couldn't believe that "bawbag cousin of ours actually pulled one of his grand plans off."

Lucas made it clear we had to leave the rave. We couldn't hang around with that much money on us. It was all over. Really over.

Lucas: "We ready? Let's get out of here."

'Lizard' by Mauro Picotto came on. To me this track was *the* trance track of all time. I know. I already told you.

But just shut the fuck up and trust me. We all have that *one* track, don't we? This was mine and they all knew it. One last track wouldn't hurt. We were all pointing to the sky.

I tilted my head back, threw my arms out wide, and soaked that fucking song in.

I was lost in the music with Cassie draped around me.

Catface started to leave.

Lucas yelled over the track at him: "We not converted you to trance yet, ya cunt?"

Catface: "Aaaah I respect the genre my good man, but I am baked like a cake so I gotta go connect with my chill."

Lucas grabbed him, shook his hand, and hugged him. Then Catface toked his fat J, and walked away, disappearing through hundreds of ravers, until he was gone from our sight.

As the track was nearing its end, a guy we knew headed our way. 'Dave the rave' everyone called him. He always wandered about on his own, selling gear, and talking about Stoicism. He had big plans to take over the world but had never been on a plane before. Anyway, he whipped out a bag of goodies from his red Adidas zippy.

Dave the rave: "Awrite troops! Want some charlie, Nathan? Got some proper white here man. Pure as the angels, just how you like it!"

I looked at the glorious white powder as the strobes lit up our faces. The gear before my wanting eyes gave me a euphoric recall. Cassie kissed my cheek, snapping me out of it.

Me: "Nah, no thanks bro. I'm already high man."

Lucas shook the duffel bag at us: "Right you two cuntos, let's get out of here."

It was pissing down again, so we sprinted back to Cassie's Mini. I can't tell you why, but as we ran the four us roared with laughter. You could say it was relief. Whatever it was, it felt like freedom.

Mikey: "Gadgies, gadgies, gadgies. We made it."

There wasn't much sleep that night. The duffel bag had another pleasant surprise in it. Fake passports for all of us. Even Cassie.

Lucas laughed to himself when he discovered them: "Catface you cunt."

When the Bank of Scotland finally sent people to officially take over the house, we made it easy for them, left the door unlocked. They arrived to find something leaning against the door. It was a black, aluminium baseball bat, with a rubber handle to grip on.

All I can tell you is when we got to our destination it was so hot that the air smothered your face. Catface had told Lucas where we were all set up and when we arrived we weren't disappointed. Within minutes we loaded most of our cash into a safe, stood on the balcony and looked at our new surroundings. We were home.

It was December so we weren't in peak season, but there was a rave starting soon, and that was our next destination.

We bought shades, and some tequila, and off we went to the rave.

We stepped out of the cab on arrival, the heat still sweltering, to the glorious sound of trance. You honestly couldn't wipe the smiles off our faces if you tried. The beach was a few footsteps away, with glistening white sand, and sea that looked so clear you wanted to get right in and taste the salty water. Before our very eyes were people full of joy and life and happiness, dancing under a tented area. That's where the beautiful track was coming from.

I wish I could tell you what the track was called, but I'd never heard this one before. I found myself hypnotised and followed the sound. It caught Lucas too. Then Mikey. I made it halfway on to the dance floor, dancing with a freedom I'd never known before. In front of us was a bar and to our right was a stage. I closed my eyes to inhale the track. Then opened them. Lucas stopped at my right. Mikey stopped at my left. The tune, I just can't explain it. It was an original. The three of us were mesmerised by it. Cassie caught us up and even she couldn't believe what she was hearing. We all looked at each other then looked over to the DJ, who stood there mixing with the biggest smile on his face, wearing yellow-tinted shades.

Epilogue

SOME MONTHS LATER

As the taxi pulled up to its destination in foggy Bathgate, the official-looking legal dude was nipping at the ears of Catface in the back. Far too many questions. The driver of the taxi was a very calm beardy guy. So calm, in fact, that he had no objections to Catface giving him a Cypress Hill CD to play for the journey as he turned the inside of the taxi into a smokeball. The taxi stopped outside of a studio. Catface stepped out followed by clouds of smoke and the annoying legal dude.

As Catface paid the very calm beardy taxi driver, he noticed the name on the side of the car.

Catface: "Cheeko's cabs. I dig it broski."

Calm beardy guy: "Cheers mate, eh. Am gonnae get more cars and drivers soon man, eh."

Catface toked a fat J: "Splendid."

The taxi drove off.

Legal dude: "OK, so, everything you need is right here. Just a few signatures to obtain from you and I'll show you around your new property. Phillip was very clear in his instructions. One set of keys only, to *Catface*—he shook his head muttering 'this is ridiculous' to himself before carrying on—and that I *must* bring you here and oversee the transaction. Though, very strangely indeed, he has advised me that there should be no other questions asked. I just can't see–"

Catface: "Yoooo legal dude, yo. You are killing my vibe here."

Legal dude: "I just have to ask. One minute he is here, the next, *poof!* What happened? Where on earth is Phillip?"

Catface grinned: "Listen, legal man, that's above your pay grade."

He toked his fat J and turned to look at his new studio. The legal dude handed him the keys and Catface signed off the paperwork.

Legal dude: "Aaah, so that's your real name. Why on *earth* do they call you Catface?"

Catface took a long toke then smiled and said: "Well compadre, that's a whoooole other story."

The end.

About the book

I am extremely proud of my memoir, *Euphoric Recall*. But I want people to know I am more than a guy with a story. I've had the storyline for *The Lost Boys of Ladywell* spinning around my head for four years. I started it immediately after the memoir came out.

This book is a completely fictional storyline with fictional characters set in the very real world I grew up in. I have borrowed heavily from characters I grew up around. But the beauty about fiction is, unlike memoir, you have the freedom to take creative liberties and mould a story of your own imagination. So, the thing about TLBOL is that some of it is utter fantasy, yet some of it is as real as it gets.

I have taken creative liberties where I needed to or wanted to. For example I mention Room At The Top or RATT in this book. This was a regular place to go clubbin and druggin for me and my mates back in the day. I have used this club in the storyline, but even fictionalised certain parts of it for creative purposes.

I have even done this with certain parts of Livingston in the story. Nothing major, just wee bits and bobs to make the story run smoother. As Chopper Read said, "Never let the truth get in the way of a good yarn."

And yet the inspiration for me writing this book is as real as it gets. Scotland is still gripped in a drugs-death crisis.

In Scotland men are killing themselves in record numbers and are incarcerated in record numbers. But more than this, it is inspired by my own experiences.

I left high school with no qualifications, no hope, no self-belief, no confidence, no purpose, no future, no industry, no chance at owning a house or buying a car or travelling the world. But what was waiting there for me was a drug-using subculture. This offered more than drugs. It offered togetherness, unity and a sense of belonging. It was amplified by music, raves and clubs.

Let me also address the music.

I will never profess to be a trance purist or anything like that. I missed the original rave movement and oh how I wish I'd been there from the start! I adore, admire and respect it.

We grew up on trance, techno, dance, dance-pop, eurodance, europop, EDM or whatever else you might call it. It wasn't all considered pure trance music. But none of that mattered to us scheme rats. Sometimes the music was all that stopped us from killing ourselves. Then came the drugs. What a combination that was.

The first time I ever really understood myself was through the lyrics to 'Castles in the Sky' after my best friend explained what the words meant for folk like us. So I couldn't leave the impact of that music out of this story, just to be considered a trance purist. This book features a bit of it all, from strictly trance music, to dance and europop and what have you.

Most importantly, this book isn't just about the music and the drugs. I won't explain here what it's all about. I want you to interpret that for yourself. But one thing I will say is the book is inspired by the people who were with me on those mad journeys. At that time we were like brothers in arms and literally felt like we were forever young.

Lastly, this book was originally called 'Where the Fuck is Phil?' and whilst I loved that name, to have Ladywell in the title just felt right. I will always love Ladywell, till the day I die.

Aidan Martin
5 August 2024

About the Author

Aidan Martin is a bestselling author, public speaker, and co-founder of the recovery organisation, The Scheme Livi, in Livingston, Scotland. His debut memoir, Euphoric Recall, was widely acclaimed. He has received an award from Authors' Foundation and K Blundell Trust towards this book. He also recently hosted an STV documentary called Let's Talk About Trauma. Aidan lives in Livingston, Scotland.

For more info visit:
www.aidanmartinauthor.co.uk

Facebook – @aidanmartinauthor
Instagram – @aidanauthor
Twitter/X – @AidanAuthor

Author Acknowledgements

I'd like to thank Julianne Ingles for the elite editing skills. Behind any good writer is an even better editor. Seriously.

Also to say thank you to Guts Publishing for giving this ballsy book a ballsy home.

Huge thank you to Authors' Foundation and K Blundell Trust for supporting me with a financial grant which enabled me to take the time to finish this book and find an agent. I am truly grateful.

I want to thank my best friend and creative partner Mark Deans for adorning this book with gorgeous artwork. I can't imagine the words without the art. And I can't imagine riding this creative wave without you.

Thanks to Ronnie McInnes for your deft touches on the digital uploads of the artwork too. I think you and Mark are the two most talented people I have ever met.

Thank you to filmmaker and friend James Reid for putting together a fantastic promo video for us.

Thank you to my brother Shayne for reading endless early versions of this and for giving me your input. There truly was no one else who could have given me that guidance. You lived through it all with me. From the good times, to the humour, to the scary times.

Thank you to my agent Jenny Todd, for always championing my work.

Thank you to my amazing wife Sam for supporting me in everything I do. You are such a selfless woman and have always supported everything I do. And to my three beautiful kids for making me the luckiest daddy in the world. I never knew my biological father, but you will always know yours.

Thank you to my incredible mum for making sure I always believe in myself. I don't know where I'd be without you.

Thank you to my dad, for being so gracious and supportive after my first book came out. As a father of three myself, I am learning more and more to be grateful for what you did for my life. Being a father is not easy.

Special thanks to John Gerard Fagan for proofreading the book and helping us to tighten it up. To anyone reading this, go and read John's book *Fish Town* (also published by Guts), it is a true masterpiece and one day they'll make the film.

Thank you to all the authors who took time to read review copies and provide such stellar reviews.

Alongside Mark Deans, I am co-founder and co-CEO of a charity called The Scheme Livi. I want to say a huge thank you to everyone who has supported the charity and to all the fantastic attendees who come along and make it the special community that it is.

Thanks to Craig-James Moncur and Stevie Creed for the filmmaking project of 2024 at The Scheme. Youz are talented cunts. Good cunts. And friends.

I really want to thank Professor David Wilson who has given me so much support since my first book came out. Thank you for the advice and the opportunities you provided me. You are a true gent.

Thank you to Sash! for allowing us to use the lyrics to 'Encore Une Fois' in the book. I love this track!

Thank you to Beverley Craven for allowing us to use the beautiful lyrics from '4 o'clock in the Morning' in this book. I am humbled by this.

Thank you to West Lothian College. You saved my life, and you educated me.

Thank you to Glasgow Caledonian University. You kept on educating me.

Thank you to recovery fellowships. You saved me too.

Lastly, thank you to Ladywell. You made me.

Aidan Martin

About the Illustrator

Mark Deans is an artist, musician, and co-founder / co-CEO of the lived experience recovery organisation, The Scheme Livi. Based in Livingston, Scotland, he is the creator of the cover art and interior illustrations in this book.

Mark met Aidan in Ladywell as a child, spending countless days playing football and watching wrestling as they grew into manhood together. Mark started making art in 2019 as a second creative outlet alongside his music. What started as a coping mechanism has since blossomed into an obsession. Alongside Aidan at The Scheme, they facilitate art workshops to help those in their community.

For more info visit:

Instagram – @darkmeansart and @markdeansmusic
Facebook – @markdeansmusic

Illustrator Acknowledgements

Mark would like to say thank you to the following people - to Rachel, my magnificent better half, for always being the voice of reason, for making me laugh every day and being nothing but an amazing support through this mad and surreal journey. To the three boys for enriching my life and showing me that I'm still very much a kid at heart. To my mum and my late dad for always encouraging my creativity from a young age and, even though it takes some convincing, for always putting faith in my ideas. To the dudes of the PHS - Robz, Ian, Deano, Pedro, Andy, Stu, Rory, Marty McFly, Dickson, Robyn and the rest, for just being the best cunts, through thick and thin. To Sue and the rest of the board at The Scheme for your never-ending faith and support. To the fantastic West Lothian College for looking after The Scheme and again, for putting your faith in us since day one. To Craig Moncur for being one of the most down to Earth folk you'll ever meet and to Ronnie McIness, one of the most creative, for EVERYTHING you have both done for us. To all of our incredible attendees and supporters of The Scheme Livi, you make my life better every day. To Julianne and GUTS Publishing, for coming back for some more and putting your faith once again in Two Lads Fae The Scheme. To my brother, Aidan Martin, for keeping the faith through innumerable storms and being by my side through the most life changing and unbelievable years of my life, here's to many more, long live this partnership and long live The Scheme Livi.

About Guts Publishing

Established in May 2019, we are an independent publisher in London. The name came from the obvious—it takes guts to publish just about anything. We are the home to the freaks and misfits of the literary world.

We like uncomfortable topics. Our tagline: Ballsy books about life. Our thinking: The book market has enough ball-less books and we're happy to shake things up a bit.

The Lost Boys of Ladywell (Oct 2024) is our tenth book.

The Transformative Power of Tattoo (Sept 2023) is a collection of fiction, nonfiction about why people get tattoos and how they transform a person's life.

Dear Mr Andrews (Jan 2023) by Lotte Latham is the true story of a young British woman's journey through the precarious landscape of sugar dating.

The Peanut Factory (May 2022) by Deborah Price is our coming-of-age 70s punk squatter memoir set in South London.

Blade in the Shadow (Oct 2021) by Jillian Halket is a coming-of-age memoir about a young Scottish woman struggling with undiagnosed obsessive compulsive disorder.

Fish Town (Apr 2021) by John Gerard Fagan is a young man's bittersweet departure from Glasgow and the next seven years of his life in a remote fishing village in Japan.

Sending Nudes (Jan 2021) is a collection of fiction, nonfiction and poetry about the various reasons people send nudes.

Euphoric Recall (Oct 2020) by Aidan Martin is the true story of a Scottish working-class lad and his recovery from addiction and trauma.

Cyber Smut (Sept 2020) is a collection of fiction, nonfiction and poetry about the effects of technology on our lives, our sexuality and how we love.

Stories About Penises (Nov 2019) is a collection of fiction, nonfiction and poetry about, well, exactly what it sounds like. To quote a prominent Australian author, 'Quite possibly the best title of the year.' We think so too.

Our website: gutspublishing.com
Our email: gutspublishing@gmail.com

Thank you for reading and thank you for your support!